I, Q SERIES

Book One:
Independence Hall

Book Two:
The White House

Book Three:
Kitty Hawk

Book Four:
The Alamo

Book Five:
The Windy City

OTHER NOVELS BY MICHAEL P. SPRADLIN

Killer Species: Menace from the Deep

Killer Species: Feeding Frenzy

The Youngest Templar: Keeper of the Grail

The Youngest Templar: Trail of Fate

The Youngest Templar: Orphan of Destiny

Spy Goddess: Live and Let Shop

Spy Goddess: To Hawaii, with Love

Spy Goddess: The Spy Who Totally Had A Crush On Me

PICTURE BOOKS

The Legend of Blue Jacket

Texas Rangers: Legendary Lawmen

Daniel Boone's Great Escape

Baseball From A to Z: A Baseball Alphabet

The Monster Alphabet

I, Q

(Book Five: The Windy City)

Roland Smith

and

Michael P. Spradlin

Sleeping Bear Press™

www.IQtheSeries.com

Copyright © 2014 Roland Smith
Copyright © 2014 Michael P. Spradlin

Library of Congress Cataloging-in-Publication Data
Smith, Roland, 1951-
The Windy City / written by Roland Smith and Michael P. Spradlin.
pages cm. -- (I, Q ; book five)
Summary: "When Quest (Q) and his stepsister Angela head to Chicago for
their parents' concert, they uncover another plot by the terrorist group
Ghost Cell in the Windy City"-- Provided by publisher.
ISBN 978-1-58536-824-2 (hard cover) -- ISBN 978-1-58536-823-5 (paperback)
[1. Spies--Fiction. 2. Terrorism--Fiction. 3. Stepfamilies--Fiction.
4. Musicians--Fiction. 5. Alamo (San Antonio, Tex.)--Fiction.
6. Mystery and detective stories.] I. Spradlin, Michael P. II. Title.
PZ7.S65766Win 2014
[Fic]--dc23
2013038500

ISBN 978-1-58536-823-5
1 3 5 7 9 10 8 6 4 2

ISBN 978-1-58536-824-2 (case)
1 3 5 7 9 10 8 6 4 2

This book was typeset in Berthold Baskerville and Datum
Cover design by Lone Wolf Black Sheep
Cover illustration by Kaylee Cornfield

Printed in the United States.

Sleeping Bear Press
315 E. Eisenhower Parkway, Suite 200
Ann Arbor, Michigan 48108

© 2014 Sleeping Bear Press
visit us at sleepingbearpress.com

For the Fays, a family of readers. Kim, LaNae,
Little Brian, Holly, and Big Brian.
—Roland

To my uncle Pat Patrick (the Wildcat) and his wife, Kathy.
For kindnesses immeasurable.
—Mike

Cast of Characters

Quest (Q) Munoz: Q is thirteen and wants to be a famous magician when he grows up. His idol is the great magician Harry Houdini. Q is ambivalent about school, but gets As in math and writing. He is seriously opposed to his new stepfather's vegetarianism and sneaks junk food at any opportunity. Tall with blond hair, he dresses the same way almost every day, usually in some variation of cargo pants or cargo shorts and a polo or T-shirt.

When Q is nervous, he shuffles cards and practices card tricks. It helps him relax and concentrate. He has a complicated relationship with his biological father, Speed Paulsen. Q is prone to premonitions, occasionally feeling that something bad is about to happen. He calls these feelings "the itch." The itch proves useful to Q and Angela on more than one occasion.

Angela Tucker: Angela, fifteen, has shoulder-length black hair with bangs, and olive skin. She has dark brown eyes and, upon first meeting her, Q thinks she is thin and a little frail-looking. But Angela is anything but frail. She wants to be a Secret Service agent like her mother, Malak Tucker, who died in the line of duty. Angela is smart, observant, and highly organized.

Angela always carries a small tattered backpack, in which she keeps extra hats, sunglasses, and other items that help her disguise her appearance when she practices her countersurveillance techniques and tradecraft (a term spies and agents use that refers to the techniques of trailing a suspect, eluding a tail, and other methods they use in performing their duties). Angela keeps her desire to be an agent secret from her father, Roger, who would not approve of her desire to join the Secret Service.

Blaze Munoz and Roger Tucker: Q's mom and Angela's dad have recently married. They are musicians and perform together as the duet Match. After marrying in a ceremony in San Francisco, they take Q and Angela on tour with them across the country.

Tyrone Boone: Boone is an old roadie (someone who travels with musicians and musical acts, performing all kinds of tasks on a tour). Boone is in charge of tour security and keeps an eye on Q and Angela. He travels with his very old, nearly toothless, and quite smelly dog, Croc. Boone is a former NOC (No Official Cover) agent for the CIA. He now uses a network of former spies to run "off-the-books" or unofficial operations.

Malak Tucker: Angela's mother and a United States Secret Service agent.

Eben Lavi: A rogue Mossad agent. (Mossad is roughly the Israeli equivalent of the CIA.) Eben is tracking a terrorist he believes is responsible for his brother's death. He believes the assassin known as "the Leopard" has a connection to Angela.

Ziv: The mysterious Ziv is a NOC agent for Mossad.

Buddy T.: Buddy T. is Blaze and Roger's manager. Though he is obnoxious and offensive in practically every way, he's still one of the most successful managers in the music business. Roger jokes that the "T" stands for "To-Do," because when Buddy talks he sounds like he's giving everyone a "to-do" list.

Dirk Peski: Dirk is nicknamed "the Paparazzi Prince" because he takes photos of the rich and famous and sells them to tabloid newspapers and gossip websites. Dirk is one of Ziv's operatives, or agents.

J. R. Culpepper: J.R. is the president of the United States, or POTUS, as he is referred to by the Secret Service. Before being elected president he served in the U.S. Senate, was vice president, and was director of the CIA.

Marie and Art: Marie and Art are Roger and Blaze's personal assistants, or PAs. Buddy T. thinks that he hired them but in fact they are highly trained agents and bodyguards working for Boone.

Heather Hughes: Heather is the president of a record company and responsible in large part for putting Match back on the charts. She knows Boone well from all her years in the music industry. Mostly her job appears to be keeping Buddy T. mollified and out of everyone's way.

P.K.: P.K. is short for President's Kid, the Secret Service code name for Willingham Culpepper, son of J. R. Culpepper. P.K. is ten years old, but smarter than most and wise beyond his years. He knows the location of many of the secret passages in the White House and has a Secret Service radio, which he uses to keep tabs on the agents so that he can practice eluding them.

Bethany Culpepper: J.R. is widowed and his daughter, Bethany, takes on the role of first lady.

Speed Paulsen: Q's biological father. Speed is a rock star and loves to play the part. He earned the nickname Speed because he could pick guitar strings faster than anyone alive. It's been a while since Speed has had any hit songs and he is jealous of his ex-wife's sudden, newfound success. Speed is annoying, hapless, confused, in and out of rehab, but at the same time strangely likeable.

Agents Charlie Norton and Pat Callaghan: Secret Service agents whom J.R. assigns to Boone's team. Both men are capable, trustworthy, and devoted to J.R. and his family.

The SOS team: A group of Boone's most trusted operatives. SOS stands for "Some Old Spooks." The team consists of:

X-Ray: The technical genius. He spends most of his time in a beat-up old van the team calls the "intellimobile." There is no computer system and no database or piece of electronic equipment X-Ray cannot hack, master, construct, or duplicate.

Vanessa: The team's designated "world's deadliest old broad." She is a master knife thrower, and Boone refers to her as a "human lie detector" due to her ability to read people and determine if they are telling the truth. Vanessa is also an exceptional driver and adept at tailing suspects without being noticed.

Felix and Uly: Formal Special Forces operatives. Given their size (both are nearly six feet eight inches tall) and matching buzz cuts, they could easily be mistaken for brothers. Their strength, expertise in hand-to-hand combat, and knowledge of nearly every type of weapon imaginable make them invaluable members of Boone's squad.

WEDNESDAY, SEPTEMBER 10 >

10:00 a.m. to 12 noon CST

Incoming

I had *the itch*. Again.

It's a feeling I get sometimes. And it usually means something unusual is about to happen. Almost always it's something bad. Like I'm about to get kidnapped. Or an international terrorist group is going to blow something up. But this itch wasn't like my other itches.

I first felt it when my mom smiled at me this morning. It was a *mom* smile. An "as soon as I get a second we're going to have a talk. And you aren't going to like it" smile. Something was up. I tried hard to think if Mom could know anything about what happened to us in San Antonio last night.

I mean the news about Sheriff Hackett and the shootings was all over the media. So of course she'd heard about that. But Boone had managed to keep *us* out of it. I don't know how. But I didn't know how Boone did a lot of stuff. Did Mom overhear something? Had we slipped up? Could she have found out that Angela and I helped stop the ghost cell from blowing up the Alamo Memorial? While she was on stage with Roger? I just couldn't see it.

So it had to be something else. But what?

Angela and I sat in the back of the private plane carrying us to Chicago. It was the next stop on the tour. She was absorbed with something on her laptop. Up in front Mom was huddled with my stepdad, Roger, their manager, Buddy T., and Heather Hughes. Heather was the president of their record company, which owned the plane. Marie and Art were sitting midway back. They were Mom and Roger's personal assistants. Actually they worked for Boone. Both of them were doing the spy thing where they noticed everything going on around them, but made it look as if they weren't actually watching anything.

Every so often Mom glanced back and made eye contact with me. The itch got worse when she did because my mom is usually pretty laid back. But something was wrong.

"Angela, I think we need to put our shields up," I said.

"Huh?" she mumbled, looking up from the screen.

"My mom is giving me the stink eye. I'm worried maybe she knows. I have a feeling that once that little meeting is over up there, we're in for . . . something."

"What? What something?" Angela asked, sounding confused.

"I don't know. That's what has me uneasy. So be ready. You're a much better liar than I am," I said.

"Uh. Thanks?" Angela said.

It was true. Angela could snap her fingers and come up with a gigantic but totally believable whopper. I was pretty horrible at fibbing. Although I had gotten better at it in the last ten days or so. Ever since we met Boone I'd gotten a lot of practice.

Boone.

Why wasn't he here? He was the best liar of all. All of this started when we picked him up in the desert at the beginning of our parent's tour. Our coach broke down at night in the Middle Of Nowhere, Nevada. Boone was sleeping outside and I nearly tripped over him when I stepped out of the bus the next morning. There he was with some camping gear and his old dog, Croc. It was a strange coincidence.

Which of course was not a coincidence at all. As a longtime roadie, Boone was experienced at all the things you needed to know to run a successful tour. But he was also a spy. And a lot more than that. Right now he was driving our parents' motor coach from San Antonio to Chicago. Along with the rest of the SOS crew, which stands for Some Old Spooks and is Boone's posse of computer hackers and trained assassins. Seriously. Assassins. Well, maybe not *technically* assassins. But Felix and Uly and Vanessa could probably get work as assassins if they wanted.

"What makes you think we're in any kind of trouble?" Angela asked.

"It's that feeling I get. Mom has been kind of weird all morning. We haven't had much chance to talk. But when we did, she was kind of short with me. Well, not short exactly. You know how parents have that tone when you've been found out? And they're trying to wait to calm down before they say anything? So they don't bite your head off?"

"Yeah."

"Like that."

Angela yawned and stretched, casually looking over her shoulder at the adults up front. Just in time to see my mom glance up and give me a stare. I had just been held hostage by a bunch of terrorists less than twenty-four hours ago. I spent most of that time terrified. But parents have a special ability to put their own unique brand of fear in you.

I couldn't take it anymore. Removing a deck of cards from the pocket of my cargo shorts, I started cutting and shuffling them like crazy. Moving them through my hands has a calming effect on me. It also bugs Angela. An added benefit.

"Do you think she saw something on the news? Or overheard something about what happened last night?" Angela was looking at me again.

I shook my head.

"I don't think so. If that were the case she would have gone ballistic already. If she had even an inkling of what's been going on she'd have scorched Boone. To the point where he would be beardless and bald. And he's pretty hairy. Remember, my mom used to be married to Speed Paulsen. She has a built-in lie detector almost as good as Vanessa's. I don't think it's that. But she's making me a nervous wreck. Her Momdar is definitely picking up something."

The group finished their little chat. Mom and Roger stood up and made a beeline to the back of the plane.

"Incoming," I whispered. Angela shut her laptop.

Mom took the seat next to me. Roger plopped down next to Angela.

"Hey, Mom!" I said, trying to sound cheerful. "How was

your meeting?"

"It was fine, Q, thanks for asking," she said. She handed me a brochure. On the front of it was a fancy-looking brick building with a lot of ivy growing up the sides. There was very fancy script reading "Haversham Boarding Academy" at the top and the caption "A Place for Learning and Growing" at the bottom. The brochure gave me an instant sinking feeling.

"What's this?" I asked, genuinely confused. I stole a quick glance at Angela. She tried to keep her expression neutral but looked a little pale.

"Well, it's interesting you should ask, Q," Roger said.

Uh-oh. Whatever had my mom up in arms, she had shared with Roger. Before discussing it with me. We were going to get double-teamed. Not good. Not good at all.

"Do you remember the deal we made about your schoolwork before we left on tour?" Mom asked.

"Uh. Yes. I remember. Most of it," I said. My breathing tightened up a little. I was instantly nervous, and when that happens, my mind starts racing. And racing. The truth of it was, after the first couple of days on the tour, we found out that Angela's mother, Malak, who was a Secret Service agent, was still alive, and she was pretending to be her twin sister, Anmar, who was one of the world's most wanted terrorists, so she could infiltrate the ghost cell. The ghost cell was a deep, deep, deep undercover terrorist network that had infiltrated the United States. The cell was going to bring the real Anmar into their leadership. When the real Anmar died in an explosion at Independence Hall, Malak, her identical twin, took her place. She'd been undercover for years now,

8

I, Q: The Windy City

trying to expose the ghost cell network. But Angela and Roger thought she died in the explosion. Then at the White House we almost got kidnapped along with the president's son, P.K., and the president's daughter, Bethany, who actually did get kidnapped. We had to help Boone and the SOS crew track her down so a team of navy SEALs could rescue her. Along the way we discovered that Boone and Croc were able to *poof!* all over the place. *Poof* is something I made up. It meant they could disappear and then reappear anywhere as if by magic. Honest. Then bombs had gone off. . . . In Texas a big-haired, evil terrorist named Miss Ruby had drugged me and held me hostage—and my hands *still* felt icky from getting pigeon poop on them in Philadelphia, and . . . whoa . . . slow down, mind. No good.

I took another breath.

We found a sheriff in Texas who helped rescue me and we got shot at with at least a million bullets by Miss Ruby and her thugs. Then, Dirk Peski, who was an undercover spy but who we really thought was a paparazzi pest, crashed his car into Miss Ruby's SUV and saved us. We had to race to San Antonio, where we crashed again, this time into a Chevy Tahoe loaded with explosives, which totally foiled the ghost cell's plot. Since all of that happened schoolwork had pretty much been the last thing on my mind. I sucked in another big breath, which only made me look even guiltier.

"Hmm. I'm not sure if I believe you, Q," Mom said. "Because this morning I received an e-mail from your teacher, Mr. Palotta, claiming he hasn't received any of your assignments in almost a week. Our deal was, you'd keep up on your schoolwork or else you'd have to attend boarding school while we finished the tour. Do you remember *that* part of the conversation?"

"Um. Yeah, but . . . I . . ."

"It's totally my fault," Angela said.

"What?" Roger said.

"What?" my mom and I said at the same time.

"It's not Q's fault, it's mine. We divided up the work. Q was taking the video and photos for the website and I was doing the research on all the places we'd visited, like Independence Hall, and I just . . . I don't know. I just got a little distracted after being in the White House and everything. And so I've been kind of moody and I'm sorry. I have most of the work done, I just haven't posted the content. I'll catch up as soon as we get to Chicago, I promise."

Angela had a really mopey look on her face and I think it caught Mom and Roger off guard. But Roger recovered. He's kind of reserved. Quiet, even. But he's a pretty good guy and he treats my mom really well.

"Angela, we didn't talk about it, but I wondered about us going to the White House myself. How it might affect you. I know what you . . . well . . . it wasn't easy for me either. But we always have to keep moving forward. And the two of you promised you wouldn't fall behind on your assignments."

Roger was referring to Angela's mother having served at the White House when she was in the Secret Service. Roger had no idea she was alive. Angela knew everything. Between having to keep that secret and worrying about her mother, Angela was getting stretched very thin. She's really smart. In the last few days I've discovered that she's also tough, capable, and a lot like her mother. Who has to be one of the most fearless people I've ever met. But Angela was also human. And she'd been on an emotional roller coaster these past few days that I couldn't even begin to imagine. No matter how strong she was, it was wearing on her. But she would never admit it.

"I know," she said, "and we'll get caught up. I promise. Once we get to our hotel–I need to finish a few things up–and I'll send Mr. Palotta the assignments."

I had learned to tell when Angela was really concerned about something. The last thing she wanted was to be sent away from Chicago. According to Boone, Malak had just been named to Council of Five, the ghost cell's highest leadership. Miss Ruby, also known as Number Three of the Five, had been taken off the board. But before Sheriff Hackett and Dirk Peski eliminated her, she sent Malak to a safe house in Chicago. She was supposed to wait there until she received instructions from Number Two. Malak would probably be happy to have us locked away in a boarding school. Angela, on the other hand, would flip out. She wanted to stay as close to her mom as she possibly could.

Mom and Roger stood up.

"All right. You've got two days to get caught up. I don't like being a hard case, but school is your first priority. Are we clear?" Mom said.

"Yes, Mom," I said. Angela just nodded while making big, sad, moony eyes.

Mom and Roger left us and walked back up to the front

of the plane.

"Whew," I said. "That was close."

"No kidding," she said.

"What now?" I asked.

Angela pointed to my backpack, which was on the floor at my feet. My laptop was sticking out of it.

"I'd say we better get caught up on our homework," she said.

Don't get me wrong. When it comes to stepsisters, I could do much worse than Angela.

But seriously, homework? How could anybody think of homework at a time like this?

Running Into Trouble

Vanessa was driving the coach while Boone rode shotgun. They were towing the Range Rover and Felix and Uly were in the intellimobile. Felix drove while he and Uly argued over who was the best running back of all time. X-Ray sat in the back doing X-Ray stuff. Boone's phone sat on the console of the coach. It was on speaker, so they were all in constant contact. Croc was curled up in one of the chairs at the dining table behind them, snoring away. Quite loudly.

"Eric Dickerson," said Felix.

"No way. Barry Sanders," Uly said. "Wait. Can I change my answer? Walter Payton. No. Sanders. Nope. Payton. Definitely Payton. Or Sanders. I'm going to have to think about this some more."

"You're both wrong," Boone said. "The greatest running back of all time is Jim Brown. He was also an All-American in lacrosse. Even made the National Lacrosse Hall of Fame."

"I still say Dickerson," Felix said. "Bigger and faster than Brown."

Boone shook his head in mock indignation. He clicked the mute button on the phone. Felix and Uly continued the argument, but Boone had a question for Vanessa.

"Why only take Q?" Boone said after a brief moment of reflection.

"What?" she asked, never taking her eyes off the road. Vanessa always paid careful attention to her driving.

"In San Antonio. They come to the hotel and snatch Q, but leave Angela behind. In Kitty Hawk, they take them both. In San Antonio, Q is moved out of the blast zone, but not Angela. Why?"

"We've all been wondering the same thing," she said.

"You have? Why didn't any of you mention it?" Boone asked.

"Because you were thinking about the next moves. You don't like to be pestered with questions when you're thinking about our next moves," she said.

"I don't?"

"Well, no, not historically. At least ever since I've worked with you. You like to suss this stuff out on your own. But we talked about it. After everything calmed down. It didn't make sense. Still doesn't."

"I know," Boone said. "It's bugging me. Q and not Angela. That means there is something about Q. And that makes me think back to Kitty Hawk. And Speed showing up out of nowhere. And how I don't believe in coincidences."

He pushed the mute button off.

"Hey, X-Ray. Remember that tracker I had you monitor in North Carolina? You got a location on it?"

"One second," X-Ray replied. "Key West," he said a few seconds later.

"Thanks," Boone said, muting the phone again.

"Huh. Something is just not adding up here. Malak has reached the very top leadership of the ghost cell. In Texas she was worried about them uncovering her real identity. And how that would threaten Angela. So they still believe she's the real Anmar, otherwise they would have taken Angela and left Q behind or killed them both to make up for losing them in Kitty Hawk." He ran his hand through his long gray hair and fiddled with his ponytail.

"Well, don't forget they *were* going to kill Angela," Vanessa said.

"I haven't. Believe me," Boone sighed, "but it's just not adding up. Killing Angela just eliminates a witness. But they planned to leave Q alive. At least as far as we know. They had to know we'd come after him. Why not kill them both? Which means, there's something about Q in this. The question is, what?" They rode in silence for a few minutes.

"Maybe we got to them before they had a chance to move him," Vanessa said. She was quiet a moment. "You look tired, Boone," she finally said.

"Vanessa, I'm more tired than you can possibly imagine," he said.

"Why don't you get some sack time? I got this. We'll be in Chicago in another few hours. And . . . whoa . . . detour," she said.

Up ahead were the familiar orange and white barrels signifying road construction. A sign with a blinking arrow directed them to the right lane. They had taken turns driving through the night. They had already passed through most of the bigger towns and cities along their route. At midmorning on this stretch of interstate there was very little traffic. Vanessa slowed the coach and turned off onto an exit ramp. At the top of the ramp an orange sign read "Detour" and pointed to the left.

They followed a four-lane divided highway for a few miles and another sign turned them onto an even smaller two-lane road. There was nothing but cornfields on either side of them.

"This is going to take forever," Boone said.

"No kidding," Vanessa replied.

Boone settled back in the seat and rubbed his eyes. Two miles behind them three black SUVs pulled out of a rutted lane in the cornfield and onto the road and zoomed off in pursuit of the SOS team.

Running Errands

Malak stood across the street from the Four Seasons Chicago. It felt good to be out of the safe house. One of the better hotels in the city, the Four Seasons was atop Water Tower Place overlooking Michigan Avenue. She sat on a bench in front of the Presbyterian church, directly across the street. As she sipped from a large paper cup of coffee, her eyes roamed everywhere behind her sunglasses. She was wearing a Cubs baseball cap, a Chicago Bulls hoodie, and jeans.

Malak was sure she wasn't being followed. All morning, after she left the safe house, she engaged in what is known in the spy game as "running errands." It was a classic countersurveillance method that allowed your backup—in this case, Ziv and his new friend Eben—to determine if you were being tailed.

Running errands consisted of just that. Normal stuff, like popping into the drugstore and emerging a few minutes later with a small bag of purchased items. Getting on the El train and taking the first transfer to a different line and making a mental note of nearby passengers who made the same move. Then getting off at the first stop after the transfer. Walking along the street for a while, then suddenly grabbing a taxi to Michigan Avenue and glancing out the rear window to search for anyone frantically hailing a cab or a car quickly maneuvering to follow. The trick was to make sudden and unpredictable moves appear normal. Otherwise whoever was tailing you would pull back and break off their pursuit.

Once there, she went window-shopping. Michigan Avenue in downtown Chicago has a section known as the Magnificent Mile, lined with dozens of upscale stores and boutiques. The reflective glass of their big windows was a perfect tool to use to check for anyone following her. She continued to pop in and out of stores and even visited a coffee shop, sitting at a table near the window for several minutes to check for possible tails.

All the while she looked for familiar people. Not so much faces, for an experienced spy would alter their appearance regularly. They would remove a coat or jacket. Obscure their face with a hat and glasses. So the Leopard looked for familiarity in behavior and movement. One trick she had learned was to watch people with their phones. Someone tailing you could change their look fairly easily, but most would use the same phone. Phones and earbuds were a good disguise for an experienced operative. Many people used them, so they tended to blend in. But changing phones every few minutes to avoid detection was problematic if they suddenly needed to snap a photo of a license plate, shoot a quick video, or call for backup. Plus phones could be traced. Spies usually used one single burner or disposable phone at a time. So Malak even studied phone and headset combinations.

It was laborious and detailed work but to save her life, she counted on her ability to notice even the smallest things. And of course Ziv was there. Always. She couldn't explain it, but in the past few years she had come to feel his presence. To sense that he was always close by and watching. She had grown anxious waiting for him to arrive from Texas. Even though Boone and President Culpepper had sent Pat Callaghan to watch her back.

While Ziv trailed after her, he observed everything that happened around her. A sedan that might circle past once too often. A certain driver he recognized who might have switched to a different car. Or a delivery truck parked in an odd location. Ziv missed nothing and was a large part of the reason Malak was still breathing.

Malak had not spotted his car even once during the entire morning. Ziv jokingly called himself the "Monkey that watches the Leopard's tail." But to Malak he was more like an old and gallant lion. She could never envision him as a monkey.

Now she sat across from the hotel, waiting for Angela to arrive.

Her baby girl. Malak was one of the most well-trained and experienced operatives in the world. When she first reconnected with Angela in Independence Hall, her heart had leaped at the sight of the proud, intelligent, and beautiful young woman her daughter had become.

But now she thought maybe she had made a mistake. Thoughts of Angela consumed her. And knowing that the cell was planning something in Chicago, and that Angela would be here—and thus in danger—was driving her mad.

"Keep doing this, you're going to get both of you killed," a voice said from behind her.

Malak calmly and leisurely sat up straight. Her hand slowly moved toward the automatic pistol secured in a waistband holster beneath her hoodie.

"Malak, don't. It's me, Pat. Pat Callaghan. I'm going to sit down on your left. So we can talk. We're just a couple of Chicagoans out for a stroll on a beautiful late-summer day. Easy now. Relax."

The bench was made of iron, painted black. It formed a square around a leafy tree that was just starting to turn autumn gold. She relaxed a little.

"How did you find me?" she asked quietly, looking down. If anyone were watching they would be unable to read her lips. She was angry with herself. How could she have missed him? Easy. Pat was Secret Service just like she had once been. They had worked together in Washington. He was one of the best agents she had ever known. Apparently he still was.

"I had a feeling you'd try to put eyes on Angela. And because it's what I would have done. If I were you," he said.

Malak said nothing. She felt a little nauseated. Pat was right. It was a horrible risk. Truth be told, she did "run errands" this morning to find out if anyone was watching her. But it was also an excuse to be here when Angela arrived. All she wanted to do was see her.

"No lecture?" she asked Pat with resignation.

"Lecture? Oh. The one where I tell you this is a good way to get you both—and maybe a bunch of other people—killed? I thought I just said that."

"That would be the one," Malak snorted.

"Sounds like you already know it. By heart."

"Pat, I–"

Malak stopped midsentence. She couldn't say anything, because he was right.

"How did you even know where Match is staying? It hasn't exactly been advertised," he asked.

"Music blogger. Wrote about his interview later today with Roger and Blaze at the Four Seasons. Took a few minutes searching to find out."

Callaghan sighed. "I *hate* the Internet."

"I appreciate you watching me until Ziv and Eben got here," she said. "I only saw you once."

"You never saw me," he said matter-of-factly. "That's the oldest trick in the book."

Malak laughed. She had, in fact, spotted his car once on the street outside the safe house. But she let it go.

"Why are you here?" Malak asked.

"For that," he said. From the corner of her eye she followed his gaze across the street as two long stretch limos pulled up in front of the hotel. The Match entourage piled out and Angela emerged from the second limo. She stood straight and stretched. Q was standing next to her and he said something that made her laugh. Malak felt the tears forming in her eyes.

"Boone and the others are on the way. Number Three was taken off the board in Texas last night," Pat said.

Again, Malak showed no reaction. But the news was startling. She had questions, but Pat had been here too long already. If someone were watching them . . .

"Things have changed slightly. Until Boone gets here I'm on Angela and Q. You need to go back to the safe house. Be the Leopard."

"But . . ." she interrupted. She couldn't help it.

"No 'buts,' Malak. Glance at your wrist like we were just having a friendly conversation. Pretend I asked you what time it is, then look at me."

She did as he instructed. And when she looked at Pat's face, he had removed his sunglasses. His eyes were bright, clear, and filled with thinly veiled ferocity.

Holding his coffee cup in front of his mouth as if he were about to take a drink, he spoke. "Anyone who wants to hurt Angela or Q will have to go through me. And I don't go down easy. She's an agent's daughter. That makes her one of ours. I've got this. Now you need to go."

He didn't need to say anything more. They were comrades-in-arms. Protecting people was their job. That protection extended to their families. Pat would die before he let anyone harm Angela or Malak.

Casually, he stood and strolled away to the street corner and waited for the light to change. She watched as he crossed, then turned toward the hotel. Angela had disappeared inside.

There was nothing left for her to do. She stood up and walked away, trying and failing to keep the tears from running down her cheeks.

New Rules

"I told you we should have stayed at the Hilton," Buddy T. shouted. Buddy T. was usually yelling about something. People in the lobby of the Four Seasons were staring.

"You only want to stay at the Hilton so you can get the Gold Club points," Heather Hughes said quietly. I often wondered where Heather found the patience to deal with Buddy T. Just being around him was exhausting.

Things got louder when the desk clerk told Buddy T. his room "wasn't quite ready." His face could turn so many different colors. He yelled a lot more, but some of the wind finally went out of him and he just threw his hands up and stormed off toward the restaurant.

We each held a room key and were about to head up to the elevators when a voice stopped all of us.

"How do you put up with that guy?" I turned around and there was Agent Callaghan. I had to remember to act surprised to see him, but Boone had told Angela and me he was coming here.

My mom spoke up first.

"Agent Callaghan? What brings you to Chicago?" she asked.

He smiled and walked up to Heather and gave her a kiss on the cheek. "I had some vacation saved up," he said. "And I really like Chicago. Thought it might be nice to spend a couple of days here."

Heather was speechless. But there was a happy smile on her face. And her cheeks colored a little bit. Back in Washington, D.C., she and Agent Callaghan had "hit it off" as I heard my mom say. And I felt instantly better just seeing him. After what happened in Texas I thought it was a good idea to have an extra set of eyes around. If he'd brought a battalion of marines with him, I'd have been downright overjoyed.

When Pat stepped through the group to get close to Heather, I noticed him do something, though. As I've said before, someday I want to be a magician. And to be a good one you have to watch people and notice their little quirks and mannerisms. Passing by Angela, Pat very quickly winked at her and the corner of his mouth lifted just for an instant. It was so brief you almost couldn't see it. But I did. And more important, so did Angela. I figured out right away that it was his way of telling her that her mother was fine. Angela visibly relaxed.

My mom is a romantic at heart. It's reflected in her music, the way she sings, and everything she does, really. She beamed from ear to ear when she saw the look on Heather's face.

"Pa—uh   Agent Callaghan, it's so nice to see you again I . . . we . . . what a surprise!" Heather stammered.

He just looked at her, and everyone was quiet, waiting for one of them to say something. Mom finally spoke up.

"All right. Let's get to our rooms and let Pat and Heather get caught up," she said.

Heather snapped right back into business mode.

"Wait, Blaze. We have the interviews and then the sound check, then . . ." Heather said, but she never took her eyes off Pat.

"Nonsense. Marie and Art can help us with all that. Q and Angela have homework, anyway, so they're going straight to their rooms." She gave us that same ominous look she'd used on the plane this morning.

"Where's Boone?" Pat asked, keeping up the charade. He knew Boone was on his way here.

"With the coach. Should be here in a couple of hours," Art said.

My mom was maneuvering Agent Callaghan into a tough spot, and, of course, she had no idea what she was doing. He was supposed to stick to us like glue. Now my mom was playing matchmaker. Boone had warned us if we tried to ditch Agent Callaghan, he'd tell our folks and pull us off the tour. But Agent Callaghan couldn't just let us go up to our rooms. And he couldn't ask Art or Marie to watch us, because they had to guard Mom and Roger. Besides, Mom and Roger thought Art and Marie were just personal assistants. They had no idea the two of them worked for Boone.

"Heather, before we grab our coffee, do you mind if I do a security inspection on all of your rooms? Just to be safe. I'm on vacation, but I'm never really on vacation, if you know what

I mean. Since Boone isn't here yet? I mean he's in charge of your security, right?" he asked.

"Oh, I'm sure everything is fine," Mom said. "You and Heather go and—"

"Sorry, ma'am," he said, "but my boss, who I believe you've met, asked me to make sure everything was okay. J. R. Culpepper is not a man you want to disappoint. It won't take long. In fact, I'll start with Q and Angela's rooms."

Pat didn't wait for an answer. He took my room key from my hand and headed toward the elevators across the lobby. We followed behind. I had a feeling once we got there we were going to get our second lecture of the morning.

All in Good Time

Eben was in a bit of a huff. They were tailing Malak all morning while she ran errands. Ziv was the most meticulous, suspicious, observant countersurveillance operative Eben had ever seen. The old man missed nothing. No car escaped his notice. No pedestrian passed by without inspection. What's more, those he watched had no idea he was observing them. Ziv seemed to have a sixth sense about which building Malak would enter, which train she would take, and where she would get off. Together, they had worked out a system over the years. Eben had still never seen anyone quite so thorough as Malak in all his days in Mossad. No wonder the Leopard had been so hard to catch.

Eben had nearly blown their cover when they were watching Malak sitting on the bench beneath the tree on the corner as Agent Callaghan approached. Eben reached for his gun with one hand and the door handle with the other. Ziv grabbed his arm before he could leave. For his age, his grip was surprisingly strong.

"No," he said. "It is only Agent Callaghan."

Eben peered down the street at the bench. He focused a small pair of binoculars on Malak and then on the man sitting next to her. The man wore a baseball cap, an oversized sweatshirt, and jeans. A large pair of sunglasses hid most of his face. But now that Eben studied him carefully, he recognized Pat Callaghan. Still, he could not believe Ziv had known who it was from this distance without a scope or field glasses.

"How did you know?" Eben asked.

"Allah blessed me with great visual acuity," Ziv answered.

Eben sighed. "Seriously, Ziv, how did you know?"

Ziv said nothing. He and Eben had been together for only a few days. They had undertaken many perils together. Ziv had actually found Eben to be a pleasant companion. But Malak was his daughter. And her life was his responsibility.

Ziv would not tell Eben he was unable to determine Callaghan's exact identity from this distance. His eyes were not that good. Instead, he watched Malak's reaction. She tensed, but almost immediately relaxed. That was the first clue. Initially, Ziv wondered if someone from the ghost cell was making contact. Had it been a threat, the Leopard would have attacked. But as Pat sat on the bench and they talked, his manner and movements, which Ziv had observed and memorized, told him who it was.

But it was better to keep a little mystery. Let Eben wonder about Ziv's nearly "mystical" powers. His daughter, his family came first. He would trust no one else with their safety.

Eben huffed. "Seriously, Ziv, how do you know?"

A few moments later, Callaghan walked away just after

the group arrived at the hotel. Malak departed shortly after. Ziv started the car.

He pulled up the arm of Eben's jacket, revealing the Omega Seamaster watch given to Eben by the president of the United States. Ziv turned his arm, making sure the light coming through the windshield glittered on the crystal face.

"All in good time, my young friend, all in good time." He put the car in gear and drove down the street to follow Malak.

Eben groaned and rolled his eyes. However, he could not argue. Turnabout was fair play.

Why Doesn't Anyone Trust Us?

We followed Agent Callaghan down the hallway to our rooms. All of us were on the same floor. Mom and Roger had a suite at the end of the hall. Angela and I had adjoining rooms next door to their suite.

Angela and I waited while Pat went in and checked for intruders. "Clear," he said from inside.

We walked into my room to find the adjoining door to Angela's room open. He was inside it, holding a small black plastic box with a bunch of green blinking lights on the top of it.

"What is that?" Angela asked, instantly curious.

"It's classified. Let's just say it makes sure no one is watching or listening." He turned slowly in a circle and waved his arm up and down. Satisfied, he turned it off and slipped it into his pocket.

"Seriously? How would they even know we're going to be here?" Angela was incredulous.

"How do they know anything? We haven't made the hotel

accommodations for Match public. But it only took your mom a few minutes on the Internet to find out you were staying here. She just watched you unload from across the street," he said.

"My mom was here!" Angela said as she rushed to the window.

"Yes, but she's gone now. And she's fine. Eben and Ziv are watching the safe house. It was pretty dangerous for her to show up here. Which brings me to my next point. I can't tell your parents that Boone asked me to keep an eye on you without tipping our hand. So here's the deal. I've got a special Secret Service tablet here in my pocket," he said. He pulled it out to show us. It was slightly smaller than the usual tablet. There were three icons on the screen and I'd never seen anything like them before. He touched one and the screen split into four smaller screens. On one of them I recognized the lobby doors at the hotel's main entrance.

"There are exactly four ways out of this hotel that won't set off an alarm. I have eyes on all four." He wiggled the screen in his hand for emphasis. "So I'm putting you on notice. Right now I'm pretty sure you're soft targets. By that I mean, I don't think the cell would risk another chance at trying to grab you. But I don't know for sure. I've been looking and watching and I haven't seen anyone actively following you. But that doesn't mean they aren't. And it doesn't mean they can't be watching some other way. Anyone inside the hotel, a room service waiter, front-desk clerk, or concierge could be part of the cell. So you've got to be cautious.

"I'm going down to the restaurant to catch up with

Heather. You're going to stay here and take it easy for a while. If you need to go out before Boone gets here, send me a text and I'll tag along. The cell tried grabbing you in San Antonio, so they're not going to be too suspicious if you go out with a bodyguard. In fact they would expect it. But I'm warning you: Do not try to ditch me. I will find you. I don't mean to come down hard on you guys. You've been through a lot. But that just means you've got to take everything seriously. So no freelancing. Agreed?"

Secret Service agents who've been on the presidential detail, like Agent Callaghan, spent most of their days instantly ready to die in order to save the life of the most powerful man in the world. It was pretty hard to say anything but yes to him.

"Okay," Angela said. The tone in her voice made me want to make sure she wasn't crossing her fingers behind her back. For once, I kind of agreed with her. I was starting to develop an aversion to hotel rooms. That happens after you've been taken from one at gunpoint. I knew Angela would rather be out scouring the city, looking in every nook for a clue or a . . . terrorist.

"No problem," I said.

"Okay," he said, giving us a little wave and heading for the door.

We stared at each other. For a moment it felt like we were really stuck. In San Antonio the ghost cell had kept a Chevy Tahoe filled with explosives in a warehouse. It gave all of us something to focus on, waiting for the moment when they made a move to use it. And Malak had found out about Miss Ruby right away. We knew who she was and what she looked like. As they say in the spy game, we had intel. Here in Chicago, we had no idea who or what we were even looking for.

"Now what?" I asked Angela.

She slung her backpack on the bed and removed her laptop.

"Send P.K. a text and find out if he's discovered anything else about our 'White House' project," she said.

"P.K." was the Secret Service code name for "President's Kid," Willingham Culpepper. After his sister, Bethany, was rescued, he'd been feeding us info on Boone he had uncovered in the National Archives. I sent him the text.

"What are you doing?" I asked Angela. Her fingers were flying over her keyboard.

"Putting our down time to good use," she said. "Looking for more information."

"Information about what?" I asked.

"P.K. has his methods. I have mine," she said. "Boone still hasn't answered all of our questions. I'm going to do some looking on my own."

One thing you can say about Angela. She doesn't quit.

"Aren't we supposed to be doing our homework?" I asked.

Angela didn't answer.

Rude Reception

"Boone, I think we got company," Felix said over the phone speaker.

Boone sat forward in the seat and peered into the coach's big side mirror. The reflection showed a black Hummer rapidly accelerating behind them. Croc jumped down from his seat at the table and trotted back and forth.

Boone watched the mirror for a few seconds, cracked open the window, and let some air in. Who could this be? Paparazzi? Some fans that wanted to follow the bus into the city? Unlikely. Somehow they had been tracked. But how? X-Ray ran sweeps for electronic surveillance and tracking devices at regular intervals on all of their vehicles.

"Easy," Boone said, "might just be a tourist. Maybe some enthusiastic fans. Hoping to get a glimpse of Roger and Blaze."

"Don't seem like tourists," Felix said. Over the phone Boone heard the ratcheting sound as Felix readied an automatic weapon to fire.

Croc huffed and then barked quietly. For just the briefest

moment he disappeared and then reappeared in the same spot. Vanessa, intent on her driving, never noticed.

Trouble confirmed.

"All right, Croc," Boone said. "Vanessa, we've got company. Keep alert. They're going to try and box us in."

"Because your dog barked? You're taking Croc's word over Felix's?" she asked. Vanessa strained to look in her side mirror but didn't have as clear a view of the accelerating vehicle as Felix did.

"Croc knows stuff."

"So does Felix."

"Very true, but . . ."

Boone never got to finish. Vanessa suddenly applied the brakes. Up ahead, about half a mile distant, two big black Suburbans leaped out of the cornfield and parked facing the coach in a V shape. A half dozen men with weapons jumped out and took up positions behind the vehicles.

"Hold on!" Vanessa shouted.

The coach fishtailed on the pavement. Vanessa steered into the skid, trying to keep it facing the blockade head on. The assault team knew what they were doing. The tour bus outweighed their vehicles by several thousand pounds. But it couldn't maneuver as well as they could. And they were experienced enough to park facing the bus, which would make it harder to break through the barricade. The heavier coach might succeed in busting through, but it would be damaged, and it could tip over or stop running. In which case the teams behind them would have a much easier time of things.

"Boone! What do you want me to do?" Vanessa shouted.

"Don't try to ram through; we're going to have to fight our way out of this!" Boone shifted his weight as the coach slowed, finally stopping no more than twenty yards from the front of the Suburbans.

Vanessa threw the coach into park and was already out of her seat, rushing to the rear. Boone crouched down below the dashboard and Croc edged forward and licked his face.

"Ready, boy?" he whispered.

Croc cocked his head, looking at Boone as if to say, "Seriously?" Then he was gone.

The windshield cracked and popped as bullets flew from a barrage of gunfire.

Caged Leopard

Malak paced back and forth in the safe house. No matter what she tried, she could not rid herself of the nervous energy she was feeling. She tried doing yoga, and meditating, but nothing worked.

"Get a grip, Malak," she muttered to herself.

Finally, unable to focus on anything else, she decided to secure the safe house. Her morning of running errands had a secondary purpose. She took a plastic bag from a Walgreen's drugstore into the upstairs bathroom. Malak had traveled the world the last few years as the Leopard. It never ceased to amaze her how many useful items could be found in an American drugstore.

She had purchased two burner cell phones. One was stored under the sink and the other was plugged in to charge. Additional items included a small bottle of baby powder, a roll of Scotch tape, and a few other toiletries.

Upon her arrival at the safe house yesterday, Malak had found the hidden surveillance cameras and microphones after an extensive search. She had also found the blind spots, which included the upstairs hallway and a few other places in the two-story house.

There is an inherent problem in wiring a house for covert observation. Too many cameras and microphones increase the chances of them being discovered. But too few devices leaves any house or structure with blind spots that can be exploited. Malak was not a prisoner or being held against her will. She was being observed. It was a small advantage, but for the Leopard, it was enough.

When she stepped out of the bathroom she thought she heard something downstairs. It was a light *click*, like a door shutting, or maybe a chair in the kitchen scraping over the wooden floor. The house had been empty when she returned. She knew this because she cleared each room upon her arrival. She took no chances.

Carefully Malak made her way down the stairs. Her automatic pistol was in her hand. The stairs descended to the front door and a small foyer. To her left lay the living room, then the dining room. The kitchen was in the rear of the house, with a back door. To her right was a coat closet. She checked and found it empty. The living and dining rooms were undisturbed. She made her way quickly through those rooms to the kitchen.

Nothing.

She checked the back door. It was locked, just as she had left it when she reentered the house.

It must be stress and nerves, she thought. *I'm hearing things.* When she entered the dining room again, there was a manila envelope lying on the table. Malak tried to remain calm. If someone wasn't already monitoring the cameras around the clock, then her reactions would be noticed when the cell reviewed the footage. The Leopard was never startled, the Leopard remained calm, the Leopard did not react with alarm. At least not on the outside.

But inside she was ready to burst. She was certain the envelope had not been there when she returned from running errands. Now there it was. And what's more, she was almost positive it had not been there a few seconds ago. On her way into the kitchen she had glanced all around the dining room. No one had been there. There was no place to hide. How could this be? She took several deep breaths.

Tearing it open she found a handwritten note with a telephone number scrawled on it and a prepaid cell phone. The note read:

Call this number. The phone is secure.

Malak dialed the number. It was answered on the first ring.

"Who is this?" she demanded.

There was no response at first. But she knew someone was on the other end. She could hear background noises and the breath of the person on the line.

"I think the question is, who is *this*?" a voice said. Whoever it was spoke into a synthesizer that disguised their voice.

"You know very well who it is," Malak said. She slipped easily into the Leopard persona.

"What I know is, until you arrived on the scene, our little organization had five leaders. First Number Five dies at the hands of a rogue agent, an attack you should have seen coming. In Kitty Hawk, you meet Number Four and a few hours later he dies at the hands of the SEAL team. Then Number Three dies under dubious circumstances. Interesting how they all died shortly after meeting you. That makes me suspicious. We have no tolerance for ambition."

"You're suspicious! I barely escaped alive after meeting your 'Number Five.' I nearly died trying to save Number Four, only to find out the next day from Number Three that Four had been killed. Now you're telling me she is dead as well. How? When did this happen? Who is responsible? I want answers! Why am I here? What is the mission?" She paused, waiting several beats before she lowered her voice and continued. "I suggest you answer before the Leopard goes on the hunt."

There were several seconds of silence on the other end.

"You'll find out. When it's time. Stay where you are. Keep this phone with you at all times. You'll be contacted." The call was disconnected.

Malak lay the phone down on the table. Barely able to maintain her composure, she made her way back up to the upstairs bathroom. Once inside she closed the door.

She pounded her fists on the sink in frustration.

Counterattack

Bullets zinged through air that was full of pieces of glass and bits of automotive upholstery. Boone ducked low behind the dash and in the next instant reappeared at the rear window in the master suite. Carefully lifting his head, he peered through the window. Felix and Uly were holding their own against the four guys in the Hummer, but the intellimobile was taking a beating. The noise of the automatic-weapons fire and the smoke from the expended rounds roiled through the air. Boone ducked as several shots chewed up the rear of the coach.

Things were about to get worse. Two more Chevy Suburbans screeched to a halt alongside the Hummer. Four guys emerged from each one. All of them were carrying fully automatic rifles and knew how to use them. Felix and Uly cursed as more bullets pocked and pinged the van, and tried to fold their massive frames back inside the intellimobile. At first, Boone didn't see Vanessa. Then she stepped out of the space between the intellimobile and the Range Rover it was towing. She let fly with two knives. Both of them found targets: Two of the attackers slumped to the ground. She must have climbed out the back window of the coach while Felix and Uly kept the shooters occupied.

The shooting in the rear momentarily stopped. Either they were reloading or changing tactics. Two men stood up and fired at the SOS vehicles. Six others split into groups of three and sprinted in opposite directions to the ditches by the road, barreling into the cornfield. If they could make it far enough, they would encircle the vehicle and catch them all in a cross fire.

The cornfield was a tactical mistake on their part. It was perfect for Croc and Boone. Boone whistled. Then he cracked the window on the rear of the coach and disappeared from the bedroom. He reappeared behind one of the shooters amid the rows of corn. The man jumped when Boone tapped him on the shoulder. When he turned around, Boone was gone— and so was his rifle. Confused, he looked back to where his companions should have been, only to find them both on the ground. The last thing he saw was the butt of his own rifle connecting with his jaw.

Boone inched out toward the road. Directly across from him, he saw Croc emerge. In the next moment he looked down to find the dog at his side. The shooting from the other side of the cornfield had ceased. Boone and Croc turned their attention to the shooters in front of and behind the coach.

The problem of the two remaining men firing from their rear was immediately solved for them. The back doors of the intellimobile burst open. Boone was shocked to see X-Ray emerge with a machine pistol in each hand. He jumped down to the pavement and darted around the Range Rover, rushing toward the Hummer. Boone had no idea X-Ray could move that fast.

"My van!" he shouted as he commenced shooting. "My computers!" He screamed curses as he ran. The two men were momentarily startled by this frontal assault. "Nobody messes with my data! My equipment! You lousy terrorist sons of guns!"

Boone couldn't help but smile. The diversion allowed Uly and Felix to take out the two shooters. But X-Ray didn't cease firing until he emptied the magazine of each pistol into whatever targets he could find.

"Felix, Uly!" Boone shouted. Both men whirled, bringing their rifles up, but relaxed upon recognizing Boone. He gestured from his position to the cornfield on the other side of the road.

"Croc took down three bad guys over there. Uly, go clean up. Vanessa, make sure X-Ray doesn't shoot anyone else. Felix, search the bodies for ID. I doubt we'll find anything. I'm guessing it's a contract crew. Probably not even cell members. Use X-Ray's handheld scanner doodad to run their prints. There are three down over here, too," Boone said.

"Uh. Boone. What about the shooters up there?" Uly asked. All of them glanced toward the front of the coach, surprised that no one had fired from that position for a few moments. The assailants in the front were probably confused and uncertain at what was happening to their team at the rear of the coach.

"Don't worry. I got them."

Boone and Croc stepped back into the cornfield.

Then they were gone.

More Questions

My phone pinged in my pocket. Right after my stomach had finished a rather long, low rumble of hunger. It was close to lunchtime. I was hungry. I'm always hungry. Roger was a vegetarian. He was trying to get us all to be vegetarians. So far I had learned one thing about vegetarians. They're always hungry. So they just eat more of things like kale and artichokes. And stay hungry.

True to our word, we had stayed in our rooms with the adjoining door open. Angela was over at her desk, trying to catch up on our assignments. And looking up stuff about Boone. Which had been made easier because P.K. was sending us stuff we would never have known about Boone and his . . . I guess "secrets" is the only word.

I lay sprawled on the bed. I was absentmindedly practicing with a couple of magic scarves. My constant riffling and shuffling of the deck of cards had finally driven Angela crazy. Knowing she was under a lot of pressure, I left her alone and went into my room. There I commenced with the sprawling and making the magic scarves change colors in my hands.

The phone pinged again.

"Are you going to get that?" she finally asked with a sigh.

"Probably not," I said.

"May I ask why?"

"I'll bet it's spam."

"Text spam? Um. Q. What if it's from P.K.?"

"Oh yeah," I said, scrambling off the bed.

Getting my phone out of my pocket is a complicated process. I almost always wear cargo pants or shorts, depending on the temperature. They're the only pants with enough pockets for all my stuff. Usually three or four decks of cards, magic coins and scarves, a rolled-up baseball hat, a pair of sunglasses, a multi-tool, and whatever other stuff I might find interesting or decide I need.

Angela had tried to convince me to keep my phone in a pocket with nothing else in it. It would be easier to get to in an emergency. Or if I needed to call Boone. Or her. Or the president. But, it didn't work out so well. I need to carry a lot of stuff. Finally I fished it out from underneath a deck of cards to find P.K. had sent me a text.

"Huh. What do you know? P.K." Angela sighed again. I was only trying to keep things light. I forwarded it to Angela's e-mail so we could open it on her computer. I walked to her desk to read over her shoulder.

HI Q and Angela.

I'm in the Solarium. With Bethany. The homework cop. Doing fractions. Pfft. Made me eat tofu 4 bfast. Ugh. Here's some more stuff I found out abt the WH. Hope u guys r doing

great. TTYL. PK.

There was a link. We opened it up and it was another scan of a really old photograph. It showed a bunch of guys in blue Civil War uniforms. They were standing in front of a tent. At first I wasn't sure what I was looking at. There was a man sitting in a chair, in front of all the other men. He had a thick black beard and looked like he was in charge.

But one guy stood off to the side and a little behind the others. It was almost like he was trying to sneak out of the picture and didn't quite make it. His face was a little blurry, but the dog lying on the ground beside him confirmed it. Croc.

"Boone was in the Civil War?" I asked.

"Apparently. And quite high up—that's General U. S. Grant, commander of the Union Army. He became president after the war. I wonder how many POTUSes Boone has known?"

"I've been thinking about that. Maybe it's not Boone in these photos. I mean not our Boone. Maybe it's like his great-grandfather or great-great something or other. Maybe Boone's family has always been involved in intelligence work going way back and that's why there are all these pictures," I offered.

Angela looked at me for a few seconds. She was determined to find out who or what he was. I just wanted to know how he did what he did. It was the greatest magic trick ever. Not having a clue how he accomplished it was driving me batty.

Part of the issue between Boone and Angela was trust. Even though he'd saved our lives a couple of times already, she didn't completely trust him. Whenever I mentioned it, she'd just shrug and say she didn't know what it was, but he was keeping *something* from us. I agreed, on a certain level.

Boone wasn't telling us everything, despite what he said, but I believed he was on our side. Everybody has secrets. Especially spies.

"That would have to be an uncanny family resemblance," she said, still staring at the picture. "And it still doesn't explain Croc."

She had me there. In the previous photos P.K. had sent us—of Boone in World War Two and in Buffalo Bill's Wild West Show—Croc was right there with him. And Croc was a strange-looking dog.

And Croc did the same magic trick as Boone. *Poofing* in and out of thin air like it was nothing. The thought of it made me kind of angry. How was I ever going to be a famous magician, and perform the greatest illusion ever, if I couldn't even figure out how a dog did it either?

There was a loud knock at the door. It made me jump. Not hard to understand why. The last time somebody knocked on my hotel room door, I got taken hostage.

"Who is it?" I asked.

"It's Callaghan," came his voice from the other side of the door. "We need to talk."

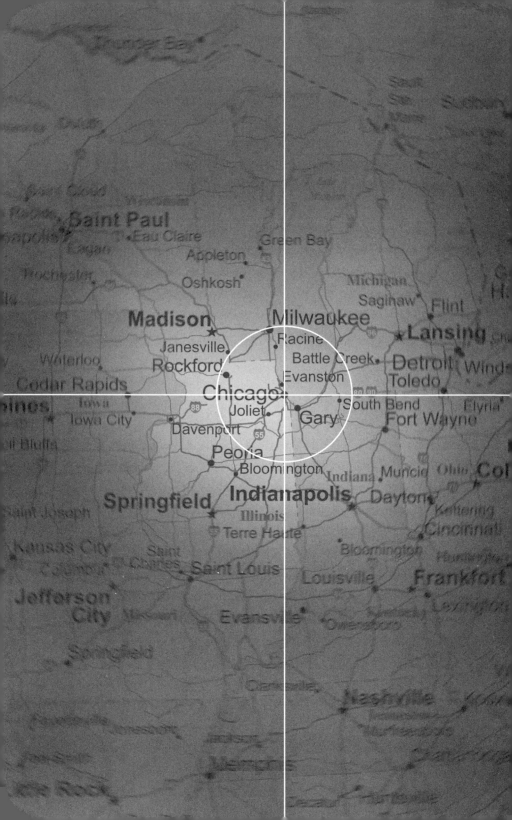

WEDNESDAY, SEPTEMBER 10 >

12 noon to 6:15 p.m. CST

We're Going to Need New Stuff

Spent shell casings were scattered everywhere on the ground. The Range Rover and intellimobile were battered and broken, with tires shot out and windows obliterated. Remarkably the coach had taken the least amount of the damage, but it was still a mess. Uly and Felix were finishing changing one front tire that had been shredded by gunfire.

Boone put his phone to his ear. It rang several times before anyone answered, but sometimes that happened. Occasionally the man he was calling could not pick up right away.

"Haven't I told you never to call during a Cabinet meeting?" President J. R. Culpepper said. J.R. didn't really speak. He gave commands. Even when he was asking questions.

"We just got ambushed. I'm going to need a bigger than usual clean-up crew. You'll need a couple of semis for the vehicles alone. Get the Illinois state police to close off this road until they get here. Make up some Homeland Security training exercise story or something that'll keep everyone away but won't make the media too suspicious. We do not want to send people into a panic. Also, I need a brand-new Marathon coach. X-Ray is going to send you the specs. You'll need to get it to Chicago ASAP, and I mean right away, J.R. If Roger and Blaze find out what's happened, we're done. They'll either cancel the tour or send Q and Angela home. If we change things up at all now, the ghost cell will disappear. And after what happened in Texas, I don't want Q and Angela out of my sight."

"Boy, Boone," J.R. said. "You don't ask for much, do you?"

Boone could hear the sound of a keyboard in the background. He knew J.R. wasn't really complaining. He wanted to destroy the ghost cell as much as Boone did. Maybe more.

"The clean-up crew is already deployed. The coach is going to be an issue. It would be easier getting you another drone on such short notice. Do you have any casualties?"

"No, just our wits," Boone said. "And a burning question. How did they know where we were? I mean, Match tour dates and venues are out there, so they knew we were on our way to Chicago. But how did they know our route? Somehow they shut down the freeway, set up a detour, and led us right into a shooting gallery."

"They've got more resources than we even thought. Boone, this is bad. I don't like this. Not at all," J.R. said.

"Me neither," Boone said.

"All right, I'll take care of things at this end. Call Callaghan and tell him what's going on and to stay alert. I've got to get back to the Cabinet meeting. You all should probably get out of there. Be careful, Boone."

"J.R.?" Boone said.

"Yeah?"

"Do you think we *could* get another drone?"

J.R. snorted and disconnected the call.

The SOS team performed their tasks with calm efficiency. Vanessa climbed aboard the coach. Boone was relieved when it started up. X-Ray had finished removing his hard drives from the intellimobile. Uly and Felix had offloaded their luggage and equipment to the coach and were now dragging the bodies of the assault team into the intellimobile. When they had pushed all of the vehicles into the corn, everyone clambered onto the coach.

"Now what?" Felix asked.

"Chicago. Then we have to figure out a way to make this coach identical to the new one, and we're going to need Q and Angela for that," Boone said.

Vanessa put the coach in gear and headed east. In twenty minutes, after a series of turns and driving down back roads, they were back on the freeway. Speeding north toward the Windy City.

On the Move

"What's the password?" I said through the door.

"Open the door, Q," Callaghan sighed.

As soon as Callaghan entered the room, I could tell by his face something was wrong.

"I just got off the phone with Boone. He and the SOS team got ambushed a couple of hours south of here. No one was injured. The coach is shot up pretty badly. POTUS is getting another one identical to it. We're going to need your help getting all the stuff off the old coach and into the new one. It will have to look right or your parents will get suspicious."

"Are you sure everyone is okay?" Angela asked.

"Yes. But Boone and I discussed it. I want you guys out of here for now. Somehow, they got eyes on the SOS crew and managed to stage an elaborate ambush. I'm probably being overly cautious, but it feels like the ghost cell is always a step ahead of us. If they could find Boone, they can find you."

"Where are we going to go?" Angela asked.

"I thought about that. You've got homework, right? Can

you sell your parents on the need to go to the library? We'll go there first. You can study. I can watch and wait to hear from Boone. After a while there, we'll move on to someplace else if Boone isn't here by then. Staying on the move is the best defense we have right now. I called Ziv. He's sending Eben to run countersurveillance on us, while he watches Malak, who is sitting tight at the safe house. Eben will call me when he's ready."

Angela had a thoughtful look on her face for a moment.

"We do have homework. I could tell Blaze we need an actual library instead of the Internet. And I've always wanted to go to the Newberry Library," she said.

"Good call. It's not too far from here," he said.

Nobody asked me where I would like to go. A library wouldn't be my first choice. But then again, they might have some magic books or Harry Houdini biographies I hadn't read yet. And then there was my recently developed aversion to hotel rooms, so getting out would be good. Pat's phone buzzed. He answered it and spoke for a short time.

"That's Eben. He's in position. We can leave as soon as you talk to your parents," he said.

We used my phone on speaker and called my mom.

"Hey, honey!" she said. My mom was almost always cheerful when she wasn't threatening me with boarding school.

"Angela is here with me and so is Agent Callaghan," I said.

"Hi, Blaze!" Angela did her best to sound cheerful and nonchalant.

"So, we've made a big dent in our homework. But we

found out that there's some stuff on Chicago history we can only get at the Newberry Library. Is it okay if we head over? Boone asked Agent Callaghan to check in on us and he said he'd go with us."

"Hello, Blaze," he said.

"Hello, Agent Callaghan," she said. She was quiet a minute. My mom is good at sniffing things out.

"Can't you wait until Boone gets here? I don't like imposing on Agent Callaghan's time and–"

Pat interrupted her. "It's really okay, Blaze. Heather is tied up on conference calls for the next couple of hours. And Boone has been to the White House a lot with other groups and he's helped me out with concert tickets before. So I owe him a favor. I don't mind keeping an eye on Q and Angela at all." He gave us thumbs up.

Mom was quiet again. I could almost hear her thinking, wondering if we were up to something. But it would be pretty hard for us to get into any kind of trouble with a U.S. Secret Service agent watching us.

"As long as Agent Callaghan is okay with it . . . I guess it's all right. But you two remember our conversation from this morning, don't you?" She said it sweetly but we knew exactly what she was referring to. Get caught up on your homework or it's off to boarding school.

"Sure do, Mom," I said.

"Yes, ma'am," Angela said. I looked at her with my eyes wide. Ma'am! She doesn't call my mom "ma'am"! It's always "Blaze." That was totally going to tip Mom off that something was up!

There were several seconds of silence. I started to sweat.

"All right," she finally said. "But listen, try to be back before we leave for the concert. I want to spend some time with you guys. I miss you."

"We will, Mom. Love you!" I said, and disconnected the call before she could change her mind.

"What conversation was she referring to?" Agent Callaghan asked.

"What with all the bombings, kidnappings, and other assorted terrorist plots, we fell a little behind on our homework. If we don't get caught up we'll be taken off the tour and sent to boarding school," I explained.

Agent Callaghan was quiet a moment while he considered this.

"Hmm. Bummer. Get your stuff. Let's go."

We got our stuff. And we went.

Walking Tour

The Newberry Library sits across the street from Washington Square Park in downtown Chicago. It took us about forty-five minutes to walk there from the hotel. It should have taken ten, but Agent Callaghan preferred a roundabout route. Every so often he would stop and pretend he was showing us something in a store window. We visited a coffee shop and he got a coffee and bought us vanilla steamers. I knew he was watching for anyone who might be following us. His sunglasses hid his eyes, but I had no doubt they studied the face of every person we encountered. But if you didn't know he was a Secret Service agent, you'd never believe him to be anything other than a dad out for a stroll with a couple of teenage kids. I started thinking he would make a pretty good magician.

Eventually we arrived at the library.

"Lots of people come here to do genealogical research," Angela said. Angela is smart and does really well with her schoolwork. If we weren't smack dab in the middle of a national security emergency, I'm pretty sure she would have been swooning. I do okay in school. But mostly I find it gets in the way of other things I like to do. Like practicing magic, eating nonvegetarian food, and avoiding being kidnapped by terrorists.

"Fascinating," I answered. "I wonder if they have any magic books."

"Seriously, Q, this is one of the world's great research libraries. Research. You know. For our school projects."

I knew Angela was referring to Boone and not our schoolwork. In addition to being smart, she's also a little obsessive. I guess we all are in our own way. I wanted to ask her, even if we found out more about Boone, how would that keep us from getting tossed into boarding school? But I decided against it. She didn't look like she was in the mood to be questioned right now.

We found a room full of tables where we could work. Angela had her laptop out and was typing away in seconds. Agent Callaghan gave us some space, sitting a few feet away, pretending to be interested in a book.

"I did some research on the Civil War picture P.K. sent us," Angela said quietly.

"Yeah?"

"It took some digging, but he comes up as Colonel A. Bertoni from the Fifth Massachusetts Regiment."

"Didn't he use a different name in the World War Two picture?"

"He did. It was Beroni. So I ran a search on Bertoni and got a couple of hits. I found an A. Bertoni on the muster roll at the Alamo. But there was no one by that name listed among the dead. Also an A. Bertoni was a clerk to a delegate at the Constitutional Convention. I ran those names through a historical-image database and guess what?" She turned the laptop around so I could see the screen. "The A. Bertoni name stops there, in the 1780s. I figure Boone changed up his name slightly every so often. Which means he must have some reason for not wanting to be found out."

"So how were *you* able to find it out?" I asked.

"I'm not sure. But the only evidence we have is what we've seen with our own eyes. Boone moving from point A to point B either like you think—by magic, which is absurd—"

"Hey!" I interrupted.

She held up her hand. "Or he moves incredibly fast. Maybe fast enough to travel through time."

"Time travel? Really? That's your guess? You pooh-pooh magic but you'll buy the idea of a time-traveling super spy?"

"Lots of scientists have theorized it's possible. And it has to do with speed. We talked about it in my introductory physics class last year. You see me sitting here because your brain processes all of the light that reflects off, around, and through me into an image on your retinas. According to some theories, if you could travel fast enough you could outrace the images out into space and see 'me' sitting here doing what I was doing a few minutes ago. Does that make sense?"

"Not at all. Are you saying Boone travels faster than the speed of light?" I asked. This particular theory was depressing. Unless I could learn faster-than-light travel, I could never pull off Boone's trick

"I don't know. But the theory would essentially be that

he moves really fast. We look up in the sky at night and see stars. What we're really seeing is the light from those stars traveling across space. Some of them are so far away the light is just now reaching us. In some cases the stars are so far away they've already gone supernova and died. But we still see the light. So the theory is, if you could travel faster than light, you could outrace what we *think* of as time and see us from any point. . . ."

"Still doesn't work. Boone doesn't go back in time. He just goes from place to place. So the time-travel thing doesn't hold water."

Angela sighed. "I know. It's not a solid theory but it is a theory. And how do we really know where he goes? When he poofs away he could go back and have lunch with Leonardo da Vinci, for all we know."

I guess Angela wasn't going to stop until she figured this out. Finding out anything she could about Boone had replaced worrying about her mom being in danger. I couldn't really blame her for that. And time traveler was no worse a theory than space alien or magical wizard or any of the other explanations we'd come up with. Best just to let it go for now.

"So I'm going to start researching names similar to Beroni, Bertoni, and others. I'm guessing Boone probably had to change his name every so often to keep people from figuring out he was the same guy, when he never aged."

"Um. Angela?"

"What?"

"This is all really interesting, but we're supposed to get caught up on our homework or we're going to get sent to boarding school."

"What do you want to do, Q? Homework or Boone?"

"What do you want to do, Angela? Tour or boarding school?"

"All right. But they have a lot of genealogical records here. I need to check something."

"Angela. Seriously. I don't think my mom is joking around," I said. I pulled my own laptop out of my backpack. "I'll help you upload stuff to the website, but we need to get caught up."

"But what about Boone?" she complained.

"I know someone who can probably help us out there," I said.

I pulled out my phone and called P.K.

Changing It Up

When they pulled into the deserted warehouse Boone saw that J.R. was as good as his word. There waiting for them was another Marathon coach. It would need to be examined carefully, but at first blush it looked identical to the one they were driving, minus the bullet holes and broken windows.

The ride to Chicago had been quiet and tense. Felix and Uly had spent the entire time in the master suite, taking turns staring out the rear window. They kept their rifles handy, but saw no suspicious vehicles.

While Vanessa drove, X-Ray sat at the dining table with his hard drives stacked in front of him. His arms were crossed and he muttered to himself. Lines of fury were still etched in his face. Boone kept his shotgun seat while Croc found a spot nearby and curled up to sleep.

Now they had something else to focus on. Along with the coach was a new Range Rover. Uly and Felix moved all the tactical equipment off the coach and into the new vehicle. X-Ray was not happy.

"What am I supposed to do, Boone?" he asked, pacing across the floor. "I can't work on the coach and the Range Rover doesn't—"

Then he saw it. The coach had hidden his view of the new intellimobile. But when he spotted it his eyes lit up. "Is that—did you—am I getting a new van?" Words failed him as he rushed to the brand-new vehicle and threw open the rear door.

Inside was a large console that sat against the wall on the driver's side. The console included four flat-screen HD monitors, multiple keyboards, and more blinking lights and equipment than anyone on the SOS team had ever seen.

Felix whistled. "Whoa, X," he said. "I bet you could invade Canada with that thing."

"Canada? I could take over the European Union," X-Ray said gleefully. He climbed into the back and sat in the black leather captain's chair in front of the console. Spinning the seat around, he grinned like a little kid. "Look!" he said excitedly. "It has a retractable satellite tower and even a periscope!" He spent the next several minutes gleefully taking inventory of his new toys before racing back to the coach for his salvaged hard drives. Once he'd retrieved them he busily went about making the new intellimobile operational.

All of them smiled, remembering X-Ray's outraged charge toward their ambushers with loaded pistols just a few hours ago. Now he was back in his element and happy. In a few minutes, monitors and lights started blinking and whirring computer noises could be heard from inside the van. X-Ray made "oohing" and "aahing" noises as the new equipment came to life.

He stuck his head out of the back of the new van and said to Boone, "You should have gotten me a rig like this a long time ago. I've been keeping everything together with bobby pins and Scotch tape." Then he disappeared inside the new intellimobile and a few seconds later they all heard him whistling as he tapped away on the keyboards.

Boone gathered the others between the two coaches.

"Okay. We need to transfer everything off the old coach. I realize things got a little shaken up during the firefight, but we have to be careful. We need it to look as close to the old coach as humanly possible. Use the cameras on your phones. Take pictures of the way the contents are arranged in each drawer. Then use the photo as a guide for putting everything away on the new coach. I know it's a lot of work, but we can't let Roger and Blaze get wise to anything. If they notice something is amiss and start asking questions—"

"Boone, even with the four of us, it's going to take a long time to move everything. We need to get some shut-eye," Uly interrupted him. Uly wasn't complaining. No one on the SOS team ever complained about anything serious. He was just stating facts.

"Don't worry," Boone said. "I was just about to call for help."

He pulled out his phone and called Pat Callaghan.

On the Move. Again.

Here's the thing. I had my laptop out, sitting across the table from Angela. To anyone observing, it would look like we were engrossed in homework. Actually it was Angela engrossed in homework. I was searching for any explanation as to how Boone could do his little *poof!* trick. So far I hadn't found anything. That was annoying.

Agent Callaghan sat down next to us.

"We've got a situation," he said.

Whenever a Secret Service agent sits down next to me and says, "We've got a situation," it makes me really nervous. Who could blame me? For all I knew, the entire library could be surrounded by ninjas. Of course, since ninjas are invisible we'd never know if they surrounded us. I couldn't help it. The last few days had made me a little jumpy. I wondered if everything in a Secret Service agent's life was "a situation." If they had dirty clothes, "We've got a laundry situation." If they needed to go to the bank, "We've got a banking situation." My mind was racing again. I needed to learn Bethany Culpepper's yoga breathing or something.

"Boone and the crew just arrived at a warehouse. The old coach was shot up in the ambush and is not repairable. He managed to secure a new, identical one. But we need you guys to go over to the warehouse now. Boone wants you to look it over. Make sure it's as close to the old one as possible," he said.

"We can do that," Angela said.

It sounded fine to me. I was happy to get out of there. Maybe it was being in a library that long that was giving me the heebie-jeebies. We packed up our stuff and a few minutes later were outside on the curb while Agent Callahan hailed a cab.

The cab dropped us at a location about six blocks from the warehouse where Boone and the others were waiting. I'd learned that being a spy involves a lot of walking. Not to mention the fact that Agent Callaghan had us double back and circle a couple of blocks a few times just to make sure no one was watching us. And even though I looked for him, I never saw Eben. So on we walked. Good thing I always wore comfortable shoes.

The building was nondescript. A battered sign that read "Security Storage" hung on the side. It looked like every other old, run-down warehouse in the area. We had to enter through a small office door at the front. Inside, it was really weird seeing the two coaches side by side. The old one looked like a brick of Swiss cheese. After seeing all the bullet holes, it made me wonder how anyone had survived.

"Wow," Angela and I said at the same time. I was instantly

happy Boone and the others hadn't been injured. Looking at the coach, it seemed like a miracle.

Everyone was busy doing something and Boone stepped out of the old coach, followed closely by Croc.

"Hey," he said, smiling. "Glad to see you guys made it okay. Thanks for lending a hand, Pat."

"Don't worry about it," Agent Callaghan said. "Jeez, Boone. What the heck happened? More importantly, how did you get through it? I've seen Humvees come through actual combat in better shape. Must have been some ambush."

"It was a little hairy," Boone said. Only he said it the same way he might have described how he'd nicked himself shaving. If Boone ever shaved, that is.

"Just tell me you got them all," Callaghan said through gritted teeth.

"Yep. J.R. sent a clean-up crew. They're taken care of. And we've got most of the personal items transferred to the new coach," he said. "Angela and Q, I need you guys to go through your berths and in particular your parents' room and see if everything looks okay. I'm trying to come up with a way to keep Roger and Blaze off the bus for a few days. But eventually they're going to be back aboard. Don't want to tip 'em off that anything's different."

Angela and I climbed aboard and did a thorough inspection. The new coach looked exactly like the old one. Boone and the SOS crew had been busy. Everything appeared to be in place. Angela's bunk was neat and orderly, the bed made. My blanket and sheets were wadded up in a mass in the middle of the bed, just how I liked them.

"Everything looks pretty good," Angela said.

"Take your time and make sure," Boone said. "Blaze is suspicious by nature, don't want her noticing anything that might make her ask questions. And some of the stuff got tossed around quite a bit in the firefight. We tried to replace everything as closely as I could remember it. Pay special attention to your parents' room. The coach was fishtailing all over the place. Anything that wasn't in a drawer went flying. Clothes got tossed around in the closet. It was a mess. It's got to be right."

We went into the master suite in the rear and that's where I found one thing Boone and the others missed. I opened Roger's closet. All of his clothes were hung neatly organized by color, the shirts on the left-hand side, the pants on the right. His shoes were lined up on the floor like soldiers standing at attention. There was a little shelf on the side of the closet that held his belts, neatly rolled up and stored. I looked at Angela and she nodded.

"That's my dad," she said. "I think that's where I get my organizational skills."

I opened my mom's closet. It looked just like Roger's, with clothes, shoes, belts, and accessories neatly stored. Which made it all wrong.

I removed a couple of Mom's blouses from their hangers and wadded them up, tossing them on the closet floor. I mixed up the hangers so the pants and dresses were intermingled. And I kicked her shoes around a bit so that no single shoe was next to its mate.

Boone chuckled and Angela just shook her head.

Done with the closet, I headed into their bathroom. Her makeup and hair products on the sink must have fallen to the floor. Whoever replaced them set them neatly on the sink, next to one another. I scattered them all over the place the way Mom normally did. And for the crowning touch, I took her bathrobe, which had been hanging on a hook on the door, wadded it up, and tossed it on their bed.

"There," I said. "Now she'll never suspect a thing."

Avoidance

The hotel lobby was chaos again. Word had filtered out that Match was staying there and the lobby was filling up with paparazzi and looky-loos. And since Mom and Roger and everyone had just returned from a round of media appearances and were standing in the lobby, everyone was getting an eyeful. And an earful from Buddy T.

We rode back to the Four Seasons with Pat, Boone, and Vanessa in the new intellimobile 2.0–as X-Ray had christened it. He sat in the back at his console and looked prepared to spend the next several months there without leaving. I had to admit it was a huge upgrade over the original. The seats were leather and comfortable. Felix and Uly ran countersurveillance on the intellimobile 2.0 as we drove the Chicago streets to the hotel. It made me wonder when any of them ever slept. Vanessa had stayed behind to guard the new coach and supervise the disposal of the old coach with the president's clean-up crew. Given that Boone could *poof* all over the place, I started wondering if his entire SOS crew might have superpowers of some kind, because they never seemed to tire. Probably not. But you never know.

We went into the hotel first, with Agent Callaghan. Mom, Roger, Heather, and Marie and Art were standing off to one side of the lobby. Buddy T. was being Buddy T. His face was red, and he was waving his arms all about. All we could hear over the lobby noise was "off schedule," "over budget," and "losing money." Buddy T. was at his loudest when it came to anything involving money.

Mom spotted us and looked relieved.

"Q, Angela! How did the studying go?" she asked, interrupting Buddy T. in mid-tirade.

"It went fine, Mom, we're almost caught up," I said. Angela was behind me and gave me a little punch in the kidney. Mom's eyes squinted at me a little bit.

"Um. Yeah. I mean. We'll be caught up real soon," I said. I had no idea when we would be caught up because I hadn't been the one doing most of the work. Like I said, I'm a horrible liar, especially when I'm put on the spot.

Mom started rummaging through her purse. "I know it's here somewhere," she muttered, just loud enough for me to hear over the noise of the lobby.

"What's here?" I asked, genuinely curious.

"Oh. Here it is." She pulled the boarding-school brochure out of her purse. The same one she showed us on the plane that morning.

"You do remember what Roger and I said, don't you?" she said.

"Uh. Yeah. But we're getting caught up and—"

"Blaze, really, we've got to deal with the schedule issue," Buddy T. interrupted. "If Q and Angela can't keep up on their homework, why don't you just send them to the school and get it over with?"

That was a mistake. Agent Callaghan, who had been talking to Heather, overhead Buddy T. being a buttinksy. Agent Callaghan didn't like Buddy T. He took the opportunity to get in Buddy T.'s personal space. Buddy T. gulped and took a step back.

"Hmm. Maybe you ought to leave what happens to Q and Angela to be decided by—you know—their parents instead of an obnoxious music manager," he said. Agent Callaghan was quite menacing when he wanted to be.

"Who are you . . . ?" Buddy T. sputtered, but his words were cut off as Agent Callaghan took a step closer to him.

"I'm somebody you really don't want to mess with."

Buddy T. was saved by Boone's arrival. "Hey, y'all," he said. "How's it hangin'?" Good-ole-boy Boone was back.

"Boone!" Blaze said. She gave him a hug. "We're glad you made it."

"Hey, Boone," Roger said. Roger did not hug Boone. Roger was not the hugging type.

Buddy T. took the opportunity to dodge around Agent Callaghan and turn his ill temper on Boone. He started right in on Boone, trying to recover from his humiliation at the hands of Agent Callaghan. "It's about time you got here. What took you so long? I'm not paying you to work banker's hours. You need to—"

Croc growled at Buddy T.

"And get that mutt out of here, I'm sure the hotel isn't going to want a stinky mutt staying in rooms that cost five hundred dollars a night. I'm not paying you to lollygag around or to clean up after some filthy dog and—"

"Actually, Buddy," Heather interrupted him, "you aren't paying Boone at all. Roger and Blaze are. So maybe you need to switch to decaf and take a break. Everyone is tired and we've got a long night ahead of us."

"I don't need this." Buddy waved his hand in the air and stomped off. Buddy T. was always storming off somewhere.

"That's my girl," Agent Callaghan said, beaming. I wasn't sure if Heather was really his girl or not, but she blushed anyway.

"I've got an idea," Agent Callaghan said. "Let's have a pizza party before we leave for the concert. There's a great Chicago-style pizza place close by, and they deliver."

"Do they have vegetarian?" Roger asked.

"I'm sure they do," Agent Callaghan said.

"Y'all go on without me," Boone said. "I gotta catch some z's." He and Croc headed for the elevator. Angela made a little frustrated hissing sound because she'd been waiting for an opportunity to get Boone's attention. She wanted more answers but he'd escaped her clutches once again.

"I could go for pizza!" I said. Hoping my mom would forget about the boarding-school issue. No such luck. I got her stern mom look. The one she busts out when she can't believe I'd really try and test her resolve.

"No pizza parties until homework is caught up," she said.

And so Angela and I passed the next few hours in our

rooms. Listening to the sounds of laughter and smelling pizza coming from our parents' suite. We were stuck doing more homework.

Roger ordered us salads from room service.

Yuck.

Everybody Talks
About the Weather

X-Ray was busy "redecorating" the intellimobile 2.0. It was parked on the street outside the hotel. He used a Chicago Public Works parking credential that clipped on to the visor to keep the van from being towed. One by one he transferred data from his rescued hard drives to the new units inside the new command post.

X-Ray was overjoyed with the new equipment. Boone must have pulled some giant strings. X-Ray was pretty sure the computers he was now using were highly classified. You certainly couldn't pick one up at your local electronics store.

Once all the data had been transferred from his old hard drives, X-Ray ran a special program he'd written to wipe them *completely* clean. Nothing entered on a computer was ever truly erased. Except with his program. Once it ran, the hard drives were effectively destroyed. He set them aside. Later he would completely disassemble them and have them melted down for scrap.

After he restored all his files from the hard drives, he

turned his attention to the data he'd stored on the cloud. Only X-Ray's cloud was not like a normal person's, where music and movies were stored. It was more like a part of his private atmosphere.

And that was when the idea hit him.

Atmosphere.

X-Ray reached into his duffel bag, where he kept a spare laptop and other gear. He found the iPhone Q had filched from Miss Ruby at the Firebrand Ranch in Texas. The phone logs, contacts, and call records were all encrypted. X-Ray had uploaded all of the phone data several hours earlier. He was running it all through a decryption program. Given his previous experience with the ghost cell, he realized it was unlikely he'd uncover anything usable. The numbers would be to burner phones or public phones in airports or bus stations. But he still went through the exercise.

However, the interesting thing about Miss Ruby's phone was that it contained several dozen photographs of Chicago. Images of the buildings, streets, and parks were intermingled with pictures of some of the city's most famous skyscrapers. In addition to the ordinary photographs that looked like they could be from a normal sightseeing trip, there were a couple that stood out.

Somehow Miss Ruby had gotten aerial views of the rooftops of the Sears Tower, the John Hancock Center building, and several other pictures of Chicago's tallest skyscrapers. Why the rooftops? What was so interesting about the tops of these structures?

Atmosphere.

The word kept tugging at X-Ray's thoughts. The ghost cell thus far had used a variety of explosive devices, mostly car bombs. Could they be planning an attempt to take down a building? How? The logistics, the security issues, and access to the buildings would be difficult to overcome. A car bomb was mobile, could be parked anywhere and positioned to create mass causalities.

Unless.

The atmosphere.

X-Ray scrolled through the photos again.

Chicago was nicknamed the Windy City. Most people mistakenly thought it was because of the strong winds that blew off of Lake Michigan. And that was part of the reason. But the nickname actually came from the nineteenth century. Back then America was growing and cities competed against each other for businesses to locate in their area. Chicago sent out politicians, bankers, and city boosters to try and attract investment in their burgeoning city. But rival promoters from cities like St. Louis or Cincinnati would tell investors anyone from Chicago was "full of wind." The nickname stuck.

X-Ray studied the photographs again, pulling up only the ones showing the rooftops of the skyscrapers. In all of the images, the sparkling blue lake was clearly visible in the background. The lake. Where the wind came from.

X-Ray had earned his nickname from Boone. Until he'd worked with the SOS crew, his colleagues had just referred to him as Ray. But Boone once said, on a job many years ago, that Ray could "see through data, like an X-ray machine." And the nickname stuck.

The wind. The atmosphere. The data.

X-Ray bent over the keyboard and pulled up weather maps. He dug into the National Weather Service database and started studying average wind velocity, wind patterns, and the seasonal effects of temperature and precipitation in Chicago.

The photos on Miss Ruby's phone meant something.

X-Ray was going to find out what it was.

Clueless

Listening to everyone have fun (and even worse, smelling pizza) was making me nuts. It didn't seem to bother Angela. I guess we still had a lot of homework. I had sent all my photos and videos from my phone to Angela. For the last few hours she had been working on updating the website.

Being caged up in the hotel room was driving me bananas. As I may have mentioned, I was no longer comfortable in hotel rooms. A good kidnapping from a hotel room will change your views on them completely.

While Angela worked at her laptop, I paced in my room. As I wore a groove in the carpet, I did coin tricks with my magic coins. And that led me to compiling a list. Making up lists is another thing I do when I get antsy. I don't know why I was so jumpy. Aside from the terrorists and stuff, I mean. Right at that particular moment, I shouldn't have been so uptight. Mom always tried to teach me that sometimes you're able to calm yourself if you make a list of what's bothering you. Then you try to work your way through it.

So I mentally compiled a record of things that had bothered me the last few days:

Being kidnapped.

Having a knife pointed at my throat.

Held at gunpoint by some really scary terrorists. Twice.

Getting pigeon poop on my hands.

Being threatened with boarding school. (This might move nearer to the top. School is bad enough. But this is a school where you actually have to *live* there. All. The. Time.)

Traveling down the interstate behind a car loaded with about a gazillion pounds of high explosives.

Being drugged by terrorists.

Stuck in a coach for long hours with the world's smelliest dog.

Having to eat Roger's vegetarian diet. (One that might also get moved closer to the top.)

A knock sounded at the door to Angela's room.

"Would you mind getting that," she muttered from her desk.

"Yes," I said.

"What? Why?" I hollered at her, a little annoyed. "Because the last time I answered the door in a hotel I got kidnapped."

"No, the last time you answered the door it was Agent Callaghan. Remember?"

Oh yeah. Details.

I sighed and went to the door. Through the peephole I saw my mom and Roger waiting out in the hallway.

"Who is it?" I said.

"Open up, Q. It's your mom and Roger," she said.

I wanted to ask them for ID. Seriously, I *knew* it was Mom and Roger. But jeez-o-pete, with my luck, since we'd learned that Boone and Croc could *poof* all over the place, how was I to know the ghost cell didn't employ shape-shifters? Maybe shape-shifter Mom and Roger had taken out Marie and Art. Not-Really-The-Real-Roger was here to feed us kale until we confessed. Or something.

I opened the door and they strolled in. Mom was happy and smiling. Roger was not frowning.

"Mom, Roger, I'm glad you're here. We've gotten a lot of our homework done. How was the pizza? We could smell it, you know," I said.

Angela was suddenly overcome by a loud coughing fit. For once it was my turn to give her the stink eye. After all, I *had* taken all the photos and video.

"In fact," I said, "we can show you the updated—"

"You'll never guess who we just heard from," Mom interrupted. The thing is, with my mom, I can never tell what she's up to. She didn't look mad or unhappy, but . . . careful, Q.

"You're right," I said. "I'll . . . never . . ." I tried to speak cautiously. Maybe Mom had found out something she wasn't supposed to know. If I said one wrong word, our carefully constructed deception could come tumbling down.

"Your teacher, Mr. Palotta! He just e-mailed us. You're all caught up on your homework. Not only that, he says it's a 'spectacular' effort. That was his word—*spectacular*."

"We are?" I asked.

Mom and Roger looked at me quizzically and Angela

coughed again in warning.

"Are you getting a cough, sweetie?" Mom asked.

"Oh, no," Angela said, kind of glaring at me. "Just swallowed wrong is all."

"I meant we *did,*" I said. "Work really hard. To get caught up. With the assignments. And . . . stuff." I had no idea we were caught up. Because I thought Angela, who had been tapping away on her computer forever, was *still* catching us up. If she'd already sent in the work, what had she been doing all the rest of the time? And why hadn't she given me a heads-up?

She could have clued me in. If our homework was done, we could have snuck down to the lobby restaurant for real food while everyone else was scarfing down pizza next door. I wouldn't have had to eat a salad that tasted like feet. Or stalk back and forth making lists of why my life had been so– interesting–the last few days.

"So we just wanted to come over and tell you we're proud of you. You kept up your end of the bargain," Mom said. Roger nodded.

"We're heading over early to do the sound check and some more interviews. We probably won't see you until the concert, but Boone will check in in a while and I guess you guys are free until then."

"That's great!" I said. I had visions of finding the nearest cheeseburger.

"Okay, we'll see you at the United Center," Mom said. Everybody hugged and they left.

When the door shut behind them I spun around and

looked at Angela.

"Clue a dude in once in a while, would you?" I said.

"Sorry, I finished it," she said. "Should have told you."

"If you weren't doing homework, what have you being working on all this time?" I asked.

"Boone," Angela said, "or also known as General Antonio Beroni. Colonel Anthony Berton. And Anthony Borneo. Among other aliases. Had a very interesting e-mail from P.K. a while ago. P.K. is not like any ten-year-old I've ever met, I might add. But nevertheless. You aren't going to believe what he found out."

I was pretty sure I wouldn't.

Change of Plans

Ever since her return to the safe house the previous day, Malak had been pondering the strange appearance of the envelope. Try as she might, she could not escape the sensation that someone was toying with her. While she puzzled it over, she paced, did calisthenics and yoga, and finally slept fitfully for a few hours.

As always whenever she was somewhere unfamiliar, she did not use the bedroom or the couch in the living room. To the Leopard, there was no such thing as a "safe" house. In her line of work alliances, friendships, coalitions, and cooperation shifted like the wind. There was always the chance that whoever she was working with at the time would turn on her. It had happened several times. Those who sold her out quickly came to regret it. She trusted no one except Ziv.

Using the bed pillows, she stuffed them under the covers to make it appear she was sleeping there. She spent the night sitting up in the corner of the dining room, dozing with her gun close by. It was dramatic and quite paranoid. But it was also how the Leopard stayed alive.

In the morning she awoke and stretched. She tried putting the matter of the mysterious envelope out of her mind. But she could not. She recalled the details from when she had returned from running errands the previous day.

The envelope had not been there when she entered the house through the back door and passed through the dining room. She was positive. From upstairs, she heard the noise in the house below. It was almost certainly a door clicking open or shut. When she came downstairs to investigate, there it was. Immediately she assumed an intruder was in the house. So she cleared it room by room, gun drawn.

Someone was testing her. As she worked her way through the house, she would hear a noise or rustle in the next room. But upon entry, pistol at the ready, no one was there. She could not explain it. The Leopard did not like things for which there was no explanation.

Whatever it was that was causing the noises was no longer here. Malak shook her head. For a moment she wondered if she was losing it. The Leopard was beginning to hear ghosts.

There was a television set in the living room. The kitchen had been stocked with a few staples and she made a simple breakfast. As she ate, she watched the local news. Flipping through the channels she looked for any news story that might give her an indication of what the ghost cell could be planning. But she could find nothing.

She strolled to the front window and studied the street. Both sides of it were lined with parked cars. Somewhere among the sea of vehicles Ziv was watching. Like always.

Now he was with Eben. She wondered if they were getting on each other's nerves. Ziv was set in his ways. In what she knew of Eben, though one of Mossad's best, he was aggressive, impulsive, and driven. Ziv was quiet, patient, and capable of both inner and outer stillness for hours at a time. Not the best combination of stakeout partners.

She was so antsy she knew she needed to get out of the house. As she was changing into running shoes the cell phone rang. Malak pulled the phone from her sweatshirt pocket and answered.

"Hello," she said.

"Listen to me carefully and do not lie." It was the same electronically disguised voice as before.

"A man named Tyrone Boone. Do you know this man?"

Malak was instantly on guard. Why would Number Two be asking her about Boone?

"I have heard the name. There were stories . . . legends, really. That he was a famous NOC agent of the American CIA. But I don't believe he really exists. Tales of Boone's exploits have been around for years. If there is or ever was a 'Tyrone Boone' he is very old. Or he's a CIA fiction, a concoction of the American intelligence community to spread rumor and fear. The Leopard pays no attention to such nonsense." The mention of Boone's name had caught her off guard. All she could think of was to go on the attack.

"Why are you bothering me with this? If there even is a Tyrone Boone, he is no threat to us. I could easily kill an old man. Are we now afraid of ghosts and legends?" Malak tried to sound convincing.

There was silence on the other end for several seconds. Then the voice finally spoke.

"Never accuse me of being afraid of anything again."

More silence. Malak could barely hear the sound of breathing through the phone. As if whoever was speaking was attempting to gain control of their emotions.

"Boone is no rumor. He is real. You are correct in that he has been active in intelligence work and is quite old. Never forget that even an old lion still has teeth and claws. He *is* a NOC agent for the U.S. government."

Malak snorted. "And why would you believe such a ridiculous notion?"

"Because for years Mr. Boone worked as a . . . are you familiar with the term 'roadie'?"

"Yes. I have heard it. Someone who works in the music business."

"Correct. Mr. Boone is currently in the employ of a musical group known as Match. They are here in Chicago and were also in San Antonio. A roadie, traveling the world with musical groups, would have easy access to countries all over the world. Especially in those places where official agents of Western governments would be unwelcome. In many ways it is an ideal cover."

"What does this have to do with anything? You are wasting my time!" Malak demanded.

"We think Mr. Boone *is* still acting as an agent for the U.S. government, investigating the ghost cell. And we have reason to believe he may have uncovered crucial intelligence regarding our plans."

"Why would you think that?" Malak's throat grew tight. She nearly choked the words out.

"Because Mr. Boone is currently running a team of former spies. Yesterday we arranged an ambush for him and his companions. They survived the attack unharmed. The operation was carefully planned. Yet they prevailed without a single casualty. Mr. Boone would seem to have some kind of sixth sense about these things."

Malak gripped the phone so tightly her knuckles turned the color of cotton.

"So what if he has? The rumors and stories about this legendary Boone have been around forever. One old man—even if he is real, as you claim—is the mighty ghost cell afraid of an old man?" Malak tried to sound exasperated and impatient.

"We are afraid of no one and you will remember your place!" The synthesized voice shouted into the phone. "The cell survives and kills the infidels because we take no chances. Boone will be dealt with. However, the Chicago operation is aborted. You will remain here until tomorrow. Number One is flying in. He wants to meet with you. You are now Number Three. Preparations and discussions must be held to fill the two remaining spots left on the council of the Five. We will review candidates and discuss our next moves. You will meet me at 8:30 a.m. in Grant Park, on the east side of the Buckingham fountain."

Malak's pulse was pounding in her ears now. Things were unfolding quickly.

"Do you understand?" the voice asked again.

"Yes. How will I know you?"

"Take the phone with you. Stand at the fountain at the appointed time. Hold the phone to your left ear. Pretend you are listening to a conversation. I will meet you and take you to Number One."

The phone went dead.

Boone. Malak breathed slowly in and out, thinking quickly. The cell was planning on taking him out. And he was in charge of keeping Angela and Q safe. Which meant they were also in harm's way. She needed to get to Ziv. But she could not risk a call from inside the house.

It was time for the Leopard to go for a run.

The Leopard Pounces

Ziv and Eben sat quietly in the car. It was a silver sedan parked about one hundred yards down the street from the safe house. Eben thought this might have been the safest safe house he had ever seen. They had been watching for hours. No one had approached the house. Not a single person passed by who looked suspicious.

"Here she comes again," Ziv said. He raised the binoculars and worked the focusing wheel with his finger. An elderly woman who lived four doors down from the safe house was out walking her white Pekingese dog.

Eben raised his arm, the sleeve falling back to reveal the Omega Seamaster watch. "The woman has brought the animal out every two hours, on the dot. Like clockwork." It was all Ziv could do to refrain from putting his head in his hands.

"I do not think a woman in her eighties, owner of a small yappy dog, is an agent of the ghost cell," Eben said.

"You can never tell. It would be the perfect cover. She could be providing regular updates on the Leopard. Perhaps it is the dog who is the spy," Ziv said. "He looks so untrustworthy."

Eben shook his head in disbelief.

"You and I have seen enough in our time in the game to know that no one is to be trusted," Ziv said.

"I do not think the woman is a spy, Ziv."

"Exactly. Which makes her immediately suspect. Why else would she walk the dog every two hours, exactly?" He pointed at Eben's watch.

"Perhaps she is obsessive-compulsive and likes to stay on a regular schedule. Maybe the dog needs to stay on a regular schedule. I have heard old people like to stay on regular schedules. But you would know more about this than me," Eben said.

"What? Why?"

"In case you haven't noticed, you are old," Eben said.

"I am not that old!" Ziv complained.

"Yes, you are."

They were interrupted by the back door to the car opening and Malak tumbling inside. Both men were ashamed to admit they were startled and had instinctively gone for their guns.

"That is a good way for the Leopard to die," Eben said, though he was disgusted with himself. He had been so intent on his argument with Ziv, he had neglected to notice that Malak was sneaking up on them.

"Malak, what are you doing here?" Ziv asked. He sat up in the front seat but did not turn to look at her as she slouched in the back. Concern was etched in his face and evident in his voice. It was unlike Malak to break protocol and contact him directly.

"I just received instructions to meet Number Two at Grant Park at 8:30 a.m. tomorrow on the east side of the Buckingham fountain. It was not safe to use any of the phones inside the house. The woman with the dog is making me suspicious. I couldn't let her see me making a call outside the house. Jogging and keeping in shape are part of the Leopard's regimen. So I jogged three blocks over and around the corner and came up behind your car, out of sight of the woman and her dog. Only to find the two of you arguing like a couple of old women."

Eben and Ziv tried not to look sheepish. And failed.

"Give me the details of the meet again," Ziv said. Malak repeated the instructions she had been given.

"So, tomorrow you will join this Number Two at Grant Park and then will be taken to an undisclosed location to be introduced to the leader of the vaunted ghost cell?" Ziv frowned as he considered these developments.

"If we can follow you, we can grab both One and Two," Eben said.

"There's more. The voice claiming to be Number Two asked me about Boone. They believe he is working for the government. And that he has uncovered something about their plans here in Chicago. They are aborting their attack. But they want to hold the meeting anyway, apparently since two of us are already here. You need to get word to him that his cover is blown."

Ziv was quiet a moment. Then he shook his head.

"Boone will not relent," he said. "Regardless of whether or not he has been compromised."

"Boone will relent and get Angela and Q to safety. If anything happens to them, I will kill him myself. I told him so to his face in Texas." Malak was suddenly angry. "They already tried to ambush him and failed. What happens if they try again and Angela is in the cross fire?"

"Yes, they tried, Malak, and they failed. Miserably. Boone and his team killed every single member of the assault team. I am not ashamed to say there is no one in our . . . business . . . who is better than Boone. No one. Do not fear, he will take every precaution to keep Angela and Q safe. But he will not give up a chance to end this. Boone will agree that we must proceed as if he is unaware the ghost cell suspects him. Sending Angela and Q away will tip our hand." Ziv was patient.

Malak pounded on the back of the front seat in frustration. Ziv and Eben let her go until she composed herself.

"But they have canceled the attack—" Malak started to say.

"So they say," Eben said, quietly interrupting her.

The realization began to dawn on Malak. Maybe they were all being played.

"Go to your meeting. Be the Leopard. Stay strong. Boone and his team will make sure Angela and Q are safe. We will stop them. We must stop them. Then you will be free, Malak. It will be over," Ziv said quietly.

Malak let out a long sigh. She opened the car door, but before she left she looked at Ziv. "Tell Boone to remember what he promised me in Texas. Angela and Q are to be safe at all costs. Even if it means pulling the plug on all of this."

"Malak, you and Angela are my blood. If Boone fails to keep her safe, it will not only be the Leopard he must answer to," the old man said.

Malak left the car and jogged in the opposite direction of the safe house. She would take a circuitous route on her return. Making anyone watching think she had only been out for a run.

Ziv was silent a moment, thinking.

"What are you going to do?" Eben asked.

"What would you do if you were in my position?" Ziv replied.

Eben, unable to restrain himself, looked at his Omega Seamaster. "I think it is time to have a talk with Boone. In person," he said.

Despite the seriousness of the situation, Ziv sighed and slumped in the passenger seat. Eben started the car and pulled out onto the street.

WEDNESDAY, SEPTEMBER 10 >

6:15 p.m. to 11:00 p.m. CST

Backwards and Forwards

Backstage at the United Center it was full-fledged, preconcert organized chaos. Roadies were moving the final pieces of equipment and the instruments into place. The noise from the crowd escalated as the concertgoers filed into the arena. Boone watched over the roadies—gesturing and pointing—and a walkie-talkie appeared to be permanently attached to his cheek. He was constantly chattering into it, all the while checking a tablet. His good-ole-boy drawl was continually giving orders and commands. I couldn't figure out how he kept it all straight. He was flawlessly setting up for a major concert and trying to destroy a terrorist cell at the same time. Talk about multitasking.

Mom and Roger were in the greenroom backstage. It was like a glorified dressing room. It was the place where the musicians readied themselves and relaxed before the concert.

Once I asked my mom why it was called a "green" room since the rooms weren't usually green. Apparently it came from the early days of theater performances in London. Most of the dressing rooms in fancier theaters were painted green. The name stuck.

Most acts had elaborate requirements for their greenrooms. Their contracts demanded they had to have certain foods, the thermostat had to be set at a certain temperature, or any of a million other odd requests. Of course Buddy T. was shouting at some poor concession person that the greenroom had the wrong kind of hand sanitizer. But that's what Buddy T. does.

Mom and Roger were pretty low-key about their greenroom requirements. All they ever asked for was some bottled water and a vegetable tray. I toyed with the idea of getting one of the concession guys to switch out the veggies for a meat tray. Just to see the look on Roger's face. And also so there would be some meat to eat. But since we'd just dodged the boarding-school bullet, practical jokes were probably not the best way to go.

Angela and I wandered around backstage. I didn't like being cooped up in the greenroom. Angela was quiet and moody because P.K. had sent her a bunch of new info about Boone. As usual, Boone was busy, surrounded by people, trying to get a concert under way, and didn't really have time to talk. Or he didn't want to talk. Boone had already shared some of his secrets with us and promised to tell us everything. He just forgot the part about Angela being impatient. As far as she was concerned, Boone was responsible for keeping her mother alive. Boone and his secrets didn't sit well with her.

"Okay, I know P.K. sent you more intel. You're dying to tell someone. So spill," I said. We stood off by ourselves behind a stack of crates. Angela opened her mouth as if she were going to complain about something, but then closed it.

"P.K. got into some kind of genealogy database at the National Archives. Lots of records, deeds, birth certificates, and other stuff to comb through, but P.K. is as curious about Boone as we are. Boone, or his exact double or whatever, has lived a long time. He changed his name ever so slightly every couple hundred years. P.K. found portraits and pictures of Boone with the last name Bertoni, Beroni, and similar spellings, probably to throw people off track. I guess before computers and cameras he could just become someone else pretty easily," she said.

"Why would he do that, though?" I asked.

Angela shrugged. "Who knows? Maybe so if he ran into people who knew him he could claim to be someone else or something. But I have a bigger question. Let's just say Boone is some kind of . . . I don't know . . . magician, like you said. And he's been alive all this time. What's he been doing?"

I thought of the pictures we'd seen of Boone in the woods in a Nazi uniform, the Civil War painting, and the other stuff we'd found out about him.

"A lot, from what we know, mostly fighting," I said.

"Yeah, but why? If you could live all that time, why would you be in every single war?" she asked.

"I don't know," I said. And I didn't. "And now that I think of it, it sort of ruins the time-travel theory. Boone just has to be old somehow. If he could travel through time, couldn't he go back in time and do stuff to stop wars, like, give Hitler poison or something?"

Angela nodded. "Anyway, P.K. found this portrait that dates to the 1100s. It's of an Italian nobleman named Sir Tonye Borneo. From there until the early 1500s the name didn't change. And in all that time there wasn't a portrait or painting of him, at least not one P.K. could find. Then, he did find something," she said.

She pulled out her phone and showed me a photo of a statue. "This was on an estate that belongs to the Borneo family in Italy." The statue was Boone. But a younger version. Not the old, wrinkly model we were used to. And standing next to statue guy was a dog that looked like a younger Croc. The dog looked like Croc when he went after Speed in the coach. Younger and friskier, not old and smelly like he was now. But it was definitely him. It was an amazing likeness—for a statue.

"Huh," I said.

"That's it?" Angela said. " 'Huh'? That's all you've got?"

"Well, no. I have a lot of questions, like how P.K. found out all this stuff. But it still doesn't explain the *poof!* or *what* he is."

"Well there's one other interesting factoid," she said. "Tonye Borneo? It's an anagram for Tyrone Boone."

"Huh?"

"Again? With the 'huh'?" She crossed her arms.

"I wonder why he's stayed with Tyrone Boone so long now?"

"Probably because it's a lot harder to hide these days. Everything is recorded and monitored. Records are kept. You need ID. So he probably just dances around the issue when anyone brings it up. Like when he says Croc has 'good genes' or something."

We went back and forth on that subject for a while. What was Boone? A vampire? A werewolf? Maybe Greek gods really existed and Boone was the Greek god of roadies? Now that Angela had traced Boone all the way back to the 1100s it just gave her something else to be frustrated about. Was that when Boone started living forever? Or did he go back even further, to ancient Rome or something? It was a lot to think about when we already had a lot to think about. Like not getting kidnapped again. Or trying to figure out the ghost cell's next move. Out came the deck of cards and I started shuffling. We just stood there a while, thinking and kind of zoning out. I think our brains needed a vacation. I was pretty sure mine did.

About thirty minutes before the concert started Eben showed up backstage. It was a little shocking seeing him there. Truthfully, he still made me a little uneasy. After all, he had held a knife to my throat in Philadelphia. Which was near the top of my list of things I really didn't care for.

Boone hustled him and us into a nearby empty office.

And he told us what they had learned.

High Stakes

"I left Ziv at one of the other cars we're using," Eben said. "He is cautious and said he fears our communications may be compromised. Personally, I think he just needed some alone time."

"Where is my mom?" Angela asked.

"She's fine. Ziv is watching her now. But there is news. Someone claiming to be Number Two contacted Malak. She was told the 'operation' they planned to undertake here has been called off. And they asked her if she had ever heard of a Tyrone Boone."

"What did she say?" Boone asked.

"She told them this Boone was a legend, nothing more than a CIA concoction. And even if he were real, he would be far too old to be a threat." Eben looked at Boone. "Your cover has been blown, I'm afraid."

Boone frowned and slowly stroked his beard while he considered this information.

"But this is good news, right?" Angela said.

Eben shook his head.

"Not necessarily. I believe so. Ziv is, well, he is Ziv. Suspicious. Malak has been instructed to meet Number Two at Grant Park at 8:30 a.m. tomorrow. Then she will be taken to meet Number One. And they will choose the next two members of their council of Five. For whatever reason, it sounds like a setup to Ziv."

"I agree," Boone said.

"What? Why?" Angela asked. "They failed in San Antonio. You said they always pull back and go to ground when something goes wrong. Isn't that what they're doing?"

"Usually. But they're *not* going to ground. If they were following their usual pattern, they'd just disappear. For a while, anyway. They don't need to meet in person. I doubt they do often, if at all. I think they're suspicious. I think they know we're onto them. And they either suspect Malak or they're testing her. Everything has gone wrong for them since Kitty Hawk. To them, she has to be the common denominator," Boone said.

"So you have to pull her out, Boone," Angela said. Her voice cracked and she sounded desperate. I put my hand on her shoulder.

"I can't, Angela," he said. "That's what they're waiting for. If she doesn't show for the meet tomorrow, they'll know she's not really who she says she is. Whether they know I'm tracking them or not, I have to pretend I don't know. If I disappear or pull her out, they're tipped off. And they'll find her and kill her. "

"Not if you got her away from " Angela started but Boone interrupted her.

"That's not all. I think Ziv is right. I don't think this is just about Malak. I think they're using the meeting as a distraction. They're planning something bigger than car bombs. And if Malak doesn't show, they'll have accomplished two goals. Knowing she's not who she says she is, and successfully launching another attack," Boone said.

"How do you know?" Angela asked. Her arms were crossed now and she was biting her lip.

"Because we're getting too close," he said.

"Why did they ask about you, Boone? Why did they ask my mother about you?" Angela asked.

Eben and I watched in a sort of stunned silence as Boone and Angela went back and forth.

Boone held his hands up, almost like he was surrendering.

"Angela, the truth is, I don't know the answer to that." He rubbed his hands over his hair. I remembered thinking, down in Texas, how tired Boone looked. If possible, he looked worse now. There were dark rings under his eyes and when he stood he was kind of stooped, like it took all of his energy to stand up. "What I do know is, I've been around the spy game for a long time. In and out of more places than you can count. If I had to guess, maybe somebody in the ambush crew this morning recognized me and got off a phone call before we took them out. After all, they called Malak right after they tried to hit us."

Angela just spun on her heel and left the room. The door swung back on its hinges but didn't shut all the way.

"Let's go," Boone said. "We've got work to do."

Ding Dong

As it turned out, the dustup between Boone and Angela wasn't the only drama of the night. Right before the concert started, I tracked down Angela, who was busy pacing back and forth and sulking. I talked her into coming with me to the greenroom and wishing Mom and Roger good luck.

"Sure. Whatever," she said.

When we went in, the room was packed. There was some tall, thin guy there, talking to my mom and Roger. Though he looked pretty young he had streaks of gray running through his hair. He was also holding a gigantic key, which he handed to Mom and Roger.

"I think that's the mayor of Chicago," Angela whispered.

"What do you suppose the key unlocks?" I asked. Angela slugged me in the arm.

"You did that on purpose!" she hissed.

And she was right, I did, but I knew she was stewing about Boone not calling off the op and I wanted to get her laughing. Or at least less stressed.

We got a dirty look from Buddy T. because the mayor was about to give a speech.

"Ms. Munoz, Mr. Tucker, I wanted to thank you for making the great city of Chicago one of your stops on the sensational Match tour. I'm here to present you with a key to the city and also to ask you a favor. Tomorrow, we will be holding a free concert in Grant Park. It will start in the morning and go all day. We're asking attendees to bring nonperishable food items and make cash donations as the price of admission. All the items and money will go to aid local food banks and the recent bombing victims in Washington, D.C. I would consider it a personal favor if Match would consent to being a part of the concert. We already have several groups and local Chicago musicians agreeing to perform and if we could add Match to the lineup it would—"

"Of course! We'd be delighted and honored. Just tell us where and when!" my mom interrupted. Only my mom would interrupt the mayor of a major city midspeech.

The mayor's little entourage clapped and cheered. Buddy T. was standing right next to me. He made this weird gasping, choking sound when he heard the words "free concert" and when my mom said, "we'd be delighted." I looked over at him to find his face nearly purple.

"Buddy?" I asked. "Are you okay? You look like you might have swallowed a chicken bone or something."

Buddy T. didn't answer; as usual, he pretended I wasn't there. I nudged Angela with my elbow and nodded toward him. She peered around me and had to cover her mouth with her hand to keep from laughing. At least she was smiling about something.

There were handshakes and thank-you's all around and then the mayor and his group left. Roger was still holding the giant key. I really wanted to get my hands on it. I figured I could make it part of a magic trick somehow. Turn a regular-size key into a giant key. Or something.

After the mayor left there were just Mom and Roger, Boone, Heather, Buddy, and me and Angela left in the room. As soon as the door closed, Buddy T. went off like a Fourth-of-July rocket.

"You can't do this concert tomorrow! I forbid it!" he said.

Oops, Buddy, pal, I thought to myself. *You just said the absolute wrong thing.*

My mom turned her focus to Buddy. I love my mom. She's even-tempered most of the time. But when she's mad, I mean really mad, you don't want to be around her. What's worse, she has two kinds of mad. The screaming, angry mad, and the worse mad. When she gets all quiet and almost calm. Like on the plane yesterday. Now she was still, jaw set, eyes glaring, defiant. Buddy was going to be lucky to leave the greenroom with all of his body parts still attached.

"Excuse me?" Mom said, her voice barely a whisper.

"We can't do any more of these free shows. It's going to kill our gross revenues and the next time we tour–"

"Buddy, if you keep acting like you own us, there won't be a next time," Mom said.

"Listen, Blaze, this little charity act is cute, but we are losing money an–"

Oh. Buddy.

"Buddy, you remember what I said about making all the remaining dates free? Having all the people who come to the shows just make a donation to the bombing victims?"

"Yes," Buddy grumbled.

"Open your cake hole one more time about how much money we're losing and we'll do it, won't we, Roger?" She looked at Roger.

"Yep. In a heartbeat," he said.

"You can't do this, Blaze! This schedule has already been thrown off-kilter by all of your free little extra concerts and public-service announcements! And then tomorrow you'll do a live show and everyone with a smartphone will record it and it will be all over the Internet! For free! Is that how you want it to work? You'll get no income from that music. We're not doing it. We need to get to San Francisco and get this tour back on track—"

"No," Mom interrupted him.

"What?" Buddy had his hands on his hips and was trying to stare down my mom. Good luck with that, Buddy. I think Buddy kept forgetting Mom was once married to Speed Paulsen. He'd already lost the argument. He just didn't know it yet.

Buddy gathered himself and threw open the greenroom door.

"You know what!" Buddy screamed. "Go ahead! Make the biggest mistake of your so-called careers. I don't need this. I'm out of here! I quit!" He stamped off toward the exit door.

The roadies clapped and cheered. One of them hollered, "Ding, dong, the witch is dead!"

Everyone in the greenroom was quiet for a second. Then Heather spoke up.

"Okay. So maybe I was a little off base at the beginning of the tour. When I said you'd love Buddy by the time it was all said and done, it was because he's the best manager in the business. I guess something has him rattled. He's been acting weird lately. But don't worry. This was just Buddy being Buddy. He'll be back by the end of the concert. And whoever said 'ding dong' will be out of a job. Now you guys have a show to do, so knock 'em dead."

And Mom and Roger did just that. The crowd went crazy. They had to do three encores.

Buddy T. never came back.

The Show Must Go On

No one paid attention to Buddy disappearing. At least at first. Heather just said maybe he was extra mad this time. Everyone just went into normal postconcert mode. The roadies had to work extra hard tonight. They had to break down all the equipment at the arena, then set up for the Grant Park show. The other truck with the duplicate equipment was already in California, ready to set up for the next concert. Boone gave them their instructions because he was personally going to make sure we got back to the hotel safely—probably because he didn't trust that Angela wouldn't try something stupid. Like rappel out of her hotel window with bed sheets tied together, so she could go find her mom. I had a feeling Croc would be sleeping with us tonight. My nose twitched at the thought.

I tried very hard not to think about it, really I did. However, I kept puzzling over the fact that there was going to be a concert at the very same place Malak was scheduled to meet Number Two. And how the ghost cell always kept kidnapping people and trying to blow up stuff wherever Match was scheduled to perform. The White House, the Alamo Memorial—and now Malak was being ordered to go to Grant Park when it would be full of hundreds of . . . targets. And if *I* was wondering about it, there was no question Angela was thinking the same thing.

We were driving back to the hotel in one of the big limos. Heather once again assured everyone that Buddy would be fine.

"Sadly, this isn't the first time this has happened. Every tour, Buddy feels like he's not being listened to and he explodes and takes off. He gets over it, though. The thing is, Buddy T. loves the music business. I don't think he could survive without it. He just needs to cool down, is all," Heather said.

If you had watched my mom during the concert, you'd think she never had a care in the world. There was no indication she'd just had a big fight with her manager. On stage there was nothing but her, Roger, the music, and the audience. It was as if for that brief period of time playing, singing, and the songs took importance over anything else. I guess all great performers are like that. There's an old cliché in show business: The show must go on. That night the show went on.

When I was growing up, my mom always told me, "People come and pay money to see you, Q. If you want to be a performer you owe it to them to give the best performance you can." And Mom always appeared on stage like she had no other job to do but give the fans their money's worth. Putting troubles out of her mind while in the spotlight is probably something she learned during all those years she was married to Speed.

Offstage, different story.

"He needs to cool down, all right," she said. She was showing her angry face again. "I've got to tell you, Heather, I'm grateful to you for everything you've done. We both are." Roger was sitting next to her and patted her on the knee to see if he could defuse things a little. No such luck.

Mom continued. "But Buddy T. is a problem. I know he has a job to do. I'd think by now he'd know how to use a little . . . finesse. That screaming act is growing tired."

"I know, Blaze," Heather said. "He's temperamental. But you understand as well as I do, he's the best manager in the business. He's personally acquainted with every radio station owner, station manager, and disc jockey there is. His press contacts are second to none . . . he's just . . . he's Buddy T.," she said, as if that explained everything.

Nobody talked about Buddy T. for the rest of the ride back to the hotel. Maybe we were just tired. Or it could be we were enjoying the calm. Anyway, we made it back to the Four Seasons. Agent Callaghan was there, waiting in the lobby to see Heather. We all stood around chatting and laughing. Mom and Roger are usually a little hyped up after their concerts. Everyone was jabbering back and forth, trying to decide if we wanted to hit the sack or get some food or whatever.

"Buddy isn't answering his cell," Heather said. "I'm going to call up to his room." She stepped away to a line of house phones on the lobby wall. A few moments later she was back, a curious look on her face.

"What's wrong?" Agent Callaghan asked.

"That's weird," Heather said. "Buddy has checked out of his room."

"What?" Mom, Boone, and Roger all said at the same time.

"I don't know," Heather said. "I asked to be connected and they told me he checked out, about ninety minutes ago."

"No messages?" Agent Callaghan asked.

"None," Heather said. "I don't recall him ever doing anything like this before."

"I can't believe he would just up and leave," Mom said, sounding slightly guilty. "We've had worse arguments than the one we had tonight."

Although nobody else noticed it, not even Marie and Art, who always kind of hovered around Mom and Roger, Boone and Agent Callaghan exchanged a look. It was brief, but it was there. Eye contact, frown, raised eyebrows, and then gone from their faces in a second. But like I've said, I'm going to be a magician someday, so I look for tells.

And then it hit me.

For some unknown reason, Buddy T. was in the wind.

And I had *the itch*.

In the Wind

"Don't worry none 'bout Buddy, Heather, I'm pretty sure I can find him," Boone said.

No matter how many times I heard him talk like that, the good-ole-boy drawl was always disconcerting.

"How would you do that, Boone?" Heather asked.

"Oh, I've worked with ole Buddy a long time. Like you said, ain't the first time he tore out in a huff like this. I 'spect he's in a bar somewhere, coolin' off. He'll be back, hat in hand, soon enough."

We all went to our rooms, mainly so Mom and Roger would think we were turning in for the night. The door between our rooms was open and Angela was plopped on her bed while I slumped in the chair in the corner. After a few minutes Agent Callaghan knocked on the door.

"Boone is waiting in the lobby; we're going to help him look for Buddy," he said.

I still had the itch. I couldn't for the life of me figure out why. Or why Boone would want our help in tracking down Buddy. Angela hadn't seen the look they exchanged, like I had.

"Why do we care where Buddy is?" she asked. "As far as I'm concerned it's better for everyone if he stays lost."

"Boone has his reasons," Callaghan said.

We followed him to the lobby where Boone was waiting for us outside the elevators.

Angela was still full of questions for Boone, but for whatever reason, Boone wasn't up for talking about it yet. It's probably why he sent Agent Callaghan after us. Still, she couldn't resist twisting the knife a little. As we walked across the lobby she asked Boone, "Do you know anything about the Bill of Rights?"

"What? No . . . I mean, I know that we have one and . . . why do you ask?" he stammered.

"It's for a school project on the Constitution. You've been around so long, I thought you might know some of the authors personally," she said.

Agent Callaghan laughed. "Boone is old, but he's not that old!"

"You'd be surprised," I said. Callaghan looked at me with narrowed eyes for a second then looked away.

"Let's head outside to the intellimobile and see if we can get eyes on Buddy T.," Boone interrupted. It was just like him to change the subject, and Angela looked at me and rolled her eyes. I had a feeling if Boone didn't start spilling the beans soon he and Angela were headed for a massive confrontation. Even if it meant exposing his secret to the group. Angela was so wound up about her mom she was past the point of caring what happened to him.

Luckily we didn't have to walk too far, since the

intellimobile was parked out on the street in front of the hotel. Boone knocked on the door and X-Ray let us in. I had finally gotten used to the old one. It was still a shock to see the new version. Although X-Ray had added those touches only he could. Mainly all kinds of extra monitors, keyboards, electronics gear, and stuff that looked like it belonged on some spacecraft that hadn't even been invented yet. X-Ray's grin never left his face. He sat in the chair and from the looks of all the gizmos and gadgets surrounding him, I was pretty sure he could run the entire country.

"X, I need you to get inside the hotel's security cameras and pull up footage from the last three hours. Buddy T. has gone off the grid and we need to find him," Boone said.

"Buddy T. has gone off the grid?" X-Ray repeated. "Why isn't that a good thing?"

"It's not necessarily bad. But something smells," Agent Callaghan said. "I just want to find him and ask him a few questions."

X-Ray's hands flew over the keyboards. None of us were sure exactly what it was he was doing, but somehow he did it and the lobby of the Four Seasons appeared on the screen. X-Ray scrolled and scrolled through the footage. Buddy T. never showed.

"Maybe he just called the hotel and checked out," I said.

Boone shook his head. "He had luggage. Wouldn't leave it behind."

"There he is," Callaghan said.

X-Ray slowed the video to normal speed and we watched as Buddy T. sped into the lobby. It was readily apparent his rage from the argument at the United Center hadn't dissipated at all. His face was still twisted into an angry red mass. He stomped across the lobby like a bull ready to charge. He spoke to no one, just entered the elevators and was gone.

X-Ray scrolled through the footage for the next several minutes but we never saw Buddy T. emerge.

"Could he have left some other way?" Angela asked.

"Maybe," Callaghan said. "He could have used the auto checkout on his TV and then left through one of the other exits. X-Ray, can you pull up the other—"

"Wait, go back," I said. "X-Ray, scroll back . . . back . . . right there . . . stop."

The image froze on a guy coming out of the elevator. He didn't look anything like the normal Buddy T. Buddy always wore expensive suits, with shoes made from the finest cordovan leather, a Rolex watch, and Hermes ties. This guy didn't look anything like that. He was wearing a plain blue baseball cap with a Chicago White Sox hoodie, jeans, and really bright yellow Nike high-top tennis shoes. He was also wearing glasses, which I'd never seen Buddy T. wear before. The frames were big ovals and obscured a lot of his face. But I'd been around him enough to notice his mannerisms and the way he walked. It was definitely Buddy.

"Are we sure that's him?" Agent Callaghan asked.

"He has the same walk," I said.

X-Ray pressed a button and the recording played. The newly dressed Buddy walked across the lobby and out the door. More buttons were pushed and a facial-recognition program ran over a captured image of Buddy's face and in a few seconds the words "Identity Confirmed" appeared on the screen.

"I'll be darned," Boone said. "Good catch, Q. X-Ray, get into the exterior cameras. Find out where he goes."

X-Ray reminded me of a concert pianist. He bent over the keyboard and typed faster than I thought humanly possible. His concentration was total. But a few seconds later, we had a shot of Buddy T. getting into a cab outside the Four Seasons.

"Traffic cams, X," Boone said. "Don't lose that cab!"

Now X-Ray really went to work. He hacked into the Chicago traffic cam system. Somehow he pulled up their archived footage. We followed the cab from the front of the hotel until it turned on Michigan Avenue. A few blocks away it stopped. Buddy T. got out, crossed the street, waited at the curb, then climbed into another cab. Only this time he was reversing direction on Michigan Avenue, back toward the hotel. But about a mile down the street, the cab pulled over, he got out and walked west to State Street. He went inside a Starbucks and we couldn't see him for a while.

X-Ray spent a couple minutes fast-forwarding through the recorded footage. While we waited my itch was getting worse. I don't even remember reaching into my pants pocket, but without realizing it, a deck of cards was in my hands. I was absentmindedly practicing a swivel cut. Finally, Buddy T. emerged and grabbed another cab, this time traveling up State Street toward the museums. But he didn't go quite that far. He got out of the cab, walked back to Michigan Avenue, and cut into a twenty-four-hour drugstore. We thought we'd lost him but he came out a while later with a shopping bag and hailed another cab.

"What is he doing?" Angela said.

"It's called 'running errands.' Some agencies refer to it as 'picking up the dry cleaning,' " Agent Callaghan said. "It means he's doing normal-looking stuff to make sure he isn't being followed. It's a classic countersurveillance technique."

"But that . . . that would mean . . . Buddy T. is . . ." Angela couldn't quite say it.

"It would mean that Buddy T. is a spy," Boone said.

"And we've got trouble," X-Ray said. "He's got into another cab headed toward Lower Wacker Drive."

"What's that?" I asked.

"It's a Chicago street. It feels like you're underground when you're on it. There's about a million places to hide down there. X-Ray, can you keep eyes on him?" Boone asked.

It was quiet for what seemed like several tense hours. The only sound in the van was our breathing and X-Ray's fingers clicking the keys. Finally X-Ray pounded on his keyboard in frustration.

"Sorry, Boone, it's dark down there, most of the lights don't work, some of the cameras are out. I'm afraid I lost him," X-Ray said. He sounded sad. The man took such pride in his work. He didn't like it when he couldn't come through.

"Don't worry about it," Boone said, "we'll find him another way."

"So Buddy T. is in the wind," Agent Callaghan said.

"Poof!" I muttered. Boone heard me and gave me a curious look.

And I tried really hard not to think about *the itch.*

The Martyr

Buddy T., or Buddy Tufayl, as he referred to himself, found the
van where he'd been told it would be. It was parked in a dark
corner of Lower Wacker Drive near a construction site. It was
covered in a light layer of dust. It was white with red letters
on the side that read "Citywide Plumbing." And beneath that
was a slogan, also in red, "You Don't Have To Live With A
Drip." The key was hidden in a small magnetized box under
the rear bumper.

Buddy retrieved the key and opened the back doors.
Stepping quickly inside he found everything waiting for him.
Just like Number One promised. Buddy quickly changed into
the Citywide Plumbing overalls. Buddy T. was Number Two
in the ghost cell. He couldn't help but smile as he started up
the van. The plan had worked to perfection.

As he drove he pulled out his phone and placed a call.

"I'm on my way," was all he said.

The next call would be more difficult. His instructions
were to call Number One when he had retrieved the van.

Buddy took a deep breath. While the plan had worked perfectly, something kept nagging at him. Numbers Three, Four, and Five were now dead. All of them killed in the last few days. The way the cell was structured, he only knew that they were dead. He didn't know the details, other than the sketchy accounts of the deaths of their aliases on the Internet. Number Three, Miss Ruby Spencer, was a victim of an automobile accident. Number Four, a man named Paul Smailes, was missing in the Kitty Hawk area, thought to be a victim of the violent hurricane that had recently passed through the area. Of course Number Five had died during an interrogation of the Leopard. He knew about that. But on the others the information was sketchy. If a U.S. intelligence agency was on to them, then details had intentionally been kept to a minimum. Number One had no additional specifics, or if he did, did not offer them.

What Buddy did know is that they all somehow perished within hours of meeting with Anmar, the Leopard. She was the common denominator. And frankly, she scared him. The Leopard was legendary for her viciousness. It had taken some doing, but he finally convinced Number One the Leopard had become a liability. Buddy had no desire to see her as part of the Five. Now she would be remembered as a martyr. When her body was recovered in Grant Park after the attack, the U.S. government would believe she had been responsible. But at least she would be off the board. It would allow them to go to ground and rebuild.

Buddy glanced down at the phone. Truthfully, as frightened as he was of the Leopard, Number One terrified him more.

Especially lately. Something had dramatically changed in his demeanor. For one thing, he seldom contacted Buddy directly. Occasionally he would send a messenger with a note, or Buddy would receive an untraceable e-mail telling him to buy a burner phone and call a number at a certain time. But for the past few months, he had insisted on numerous personal meetings.

These last weeks their activity and missions increased dramatically. Number One had been demanding, angry, and impatient. Buddy felt the attacks they planned were rushed, logistically problematic, and unnecessary. Trying to kidnap the president's children, for example, had proved to be a disaster.

Lately though, Buddy knew better than to question Number One. His temper had become volcanic. After the problems with the car bombs in Kitty Hawk, Buddy had argued for caution. But Number One would not hear of it. Everything was to go ahead. Plans were to proceed without delay. So Buddy asked no questions.

For now, Buddy T. went along with whatever Number One wanted. He knew the other members of the Five had viewed him as a toady. But they didn't have the experience with Number One that Buddy did. They went back a long way. Number One was just . . . *different.* There were things in Buddy's life no one should ever be able to know but somehow Number One knew them. There were times when Buddy felt like Number One was always watching. That if he turned and looked over his shoulder he would find the leader of the ghost cell standing there, peering at him.

Whenever they met in person, Buddy left the meeting

feeling uneasy. Number One would ask penetrating questions about things Buddy had done. The people he talked to, and what plans he was making. The strange part of it was, Buddy always had the feeling that Number One already knew the answers.

His palms had grown damp as he drove. But he could delay no longer. For all he knew, Number One could be watching him right now. He entered the number and pressed "send," putting the phone on speaker. The phone rang once and someone answered, but remained silent.

"It's me," he said.

"Hello, Buddy Tufayl," the voice on the other end said, "it's almost time."

"What are your instructions?" Buddy asked.

There was silence for a moment. Buddy felt a bead of sweat run from his forehead down between his eyes and along the bridge of his nose.

The voice gave Buddy his orders.

THURSDAY, SEPTEMBER 11 >

12:15 a.m. to 9:45 a.m. CST

Up All Night

Boone had Angela and me call Mom and Roger and tell them we were both beat and turning in for the night. Mom and Roger were still on a postconcert high and they were fine with it. Usually, if you call your parents to tell them you're going to bed, they're not going to ask many questions. I just hoped Mom didn't walk down the hall and check on us. I was pretty sure she wouldn't. Mom liked to revel in the success of a show for a while after it was over. As long as she knew we were safe, she'd trust us to be in our rooms. Which, of course, made me feel guilty for deceiving her. Like I said. I'm not cut out for this spy business.

Boone had Felix, Uly, and Vanessa in a vehicle patrolling around Lower Wacker Drive. Eben and Ziv were watching Malak. Inside the intellimobile it was me, Angela, X-Ray, Agent Callaghan, and Boone. And, of course, Croc, which significantly lowered the van's air quality.

The new intellimobile had a monitor for each of us. There were four main high-definition monitors. But it also had several extra monitors that folded into and out of little nooks and crannies. It seemed like every time you turned around a monitor folded up or down from somewhere. Or was built into a console and silently dropped down from the celling or something. All of us except X-Ray were watching video footage of cameras from all around the city, looking for any sign of Buddy T. Agent Callaghan was watching bus and train terminals. Boone was watching the airports. Angela and I were sorting through the major hotels to see if Buddy had holed up somewhere else.

"Why are we doing this?" Angela groused. "If he's gone, he's gone. I still don't understand why you don't just pull my mom in."

I hadn't told Angela, or anyone else, about *the itch*. Which was getting worse by the moment.

"It's got to be a setup," Boone said. "Up till now, everything the cell has done has been secretive, unexpected, and compartmentalized. Now they've lost three of their highest-ranking members in the last few days, all of whom were last seen with your mother."

"I don't follow," Angela said.

"They're going against their playbook. An ambush in the middle of the day, in a deserted cornfield? That's not their style. Then they want your mother to meet in Grant Park at a time when it will be packed with people? Not a coincidence. My guess is they knew the concert was happening when they called Malak. It's a classic case of killing two birds with one stone. If her body is discovered among the dead, it will be the Leopard who martyred herself in a deadly terrorist attack. It wraps everything up in a bow. They clearly don't trust Malak. They think she's either gone rogue or is working with me somehow."

"I still don't see where Buddy T. fits in to all of this," I said.

"If you were going to ask Match to play at a special concert, who would you call?" Agent Callaghan asked.

"Their manager," Angela said.

"Win," Agent Callaghan said, smiling.

"So his whole fit was an act?" I asked.

"That's my guess," Boone said. "He expected your parents would be asked to play, waited for the mayor to show up, and used the free concert as an excuse to get out of the danger zone."

"Do you think he's part of the ghost cell?" Angela asked.

"I don't know about that," X-Ray interrupted. "But he's clearly involved in something and he's also got a very unusual past."

"What do you have, X?" Boone asked.

"Buddy T. Born September 14, 1974. Birth mother and father died in an automobile accident. The 'T' in Buddy T. stands for Tufayl," he said, swiveling around in his chair to look at us.

"Is that important?" I asked.

"Yes," Angela said. "Tufayl is Arabic for 'baby.' "

I didn't catch the implication at first, because I was chuckling at the thought that Buddy Baby would have been a much better name than Buddy T.

"Grew up in San Francisco," X-Ray continued. "Adopted at the age of three months . . ."

"Who would adopt Buddy T.? Even as a baby?" I asked. I couldn't help it. It was too easy.

"He grew up in San Francisco," X-Ray continued. "His adoptive parents are also deceased and he's never been married."

"I'll be darned," Agent Callaghan and Boone said at the same time.

"Find out where he's going," Boone said.

"I'm on it," X-Ray said.

Croc barked.

Preparations

The Citywide Plumbing van cruised down a dark street not far from the United Center. Buddy smiled at the irony. Only a few hours ago he had staged his elaborate ruse at this very spot. Shortly everything would be in place. Then he planned to disappear. Someplace where not even Number One could find him. If such a place existed.

Buddy T. preferred not to think about that one minor flaw in his plan.

A little over half a mile past the arena he pulled off the street and into a narrow alley. At the end of the alley a slatted metal door opened into a small garage. Two men waited for him.

Buddy T. put the van in park and climbed out. None of them spoke to the others. They would communicate only as much as was needed to complete the mission. This was strict ghost cell protocol. There was no exchange of names, no small talk. Should they be captured and interrogated, no one would or could be coerced into compromising the other team members.

His companions were already dressed in the plumbing company overalls. They stood next to a large wooden crate. Stenciled on the side were the words "Commercial Backflow Preventers." The words meant little to Buddy. The top of the crate contained the actual plumbing devices, but they were interested in what lay beneath.

Number One had tasked Buddy with making a "big splash," as he called it. He wanted the ghost cell to send a statement. It was to be a coordinated assault for maximum casualties that would both shock and paralyze all of the West's intelligence agencies. As he often did, Buddy argued against it. "Big splashes" were not the ghost cell way. True, they used their attacks to maximum effect, but their entire existence had been all about deep cover within the United States—attacking, but letting other groups take credit for their work. At least it had been until recently.

Since he was not Number One, he followed orders. Try as he might he could not understand the changes taking place in the one person above him. The strange and conflicting instructions. Raising the group's profile when before they had always remained in the shadows. These things troubled him.

Buddy thought back to San Antonio. Number One had decided to have Number Three kidnap Quest Munoz and have Angela Tucker killed. Why? What did they have to do with anything? He still didn't know all the details—Number Three was dead, after all—but it had been botched somehow. Some hick sheriff, who had been at the concert to help the San Antonio PD with crowd control, had stopped the car bomb.

At least that was what he'd read on the Internet.

Yet, no matter how wrong he thought the plan was, Buddy always voted with Number One. With the way the vote was structured, it almost always ensured Number One's wishes carried the day. The other members of the Five could make fun of him all they wished. They didn't know their leader as he did. Buddy T. had been with him far longer than the others. Buddy T. feared him.

Nothing had gone right these past few days. Which is why Buddy kept pushing Number One to pull back and regroup. They had time. With better planning and more caution they could strike a heavier blow against their enemies. But his words were ignored.

Oh, well. Buddy T. had not become the best manager in the music business without knowing how to negotiate his way out of a tight situation. He pulled up the sleeve on his coveralls and looked at his Rolex. He loved that watch. It had cost him thousands and it had a bright-red stainless steel band. Being around rock stars and musicians for most of his adult life had given him an appreciation for the finer things. He would hate to give it up. The thought that he could easily afford another one made him smile.

He glanced at his companions. They didn't know it, but one of them was going to die tonight. And furthermore, one of them was going to *become* Buddy T. His charred remains would be found in the burned-out van, which would be ditched after they were finished. A bright-red Rolex around his wrist, and Buddy T.'s ID in his pocket. He knew the ruse would not stand up to long-term investigation. Eventually they would conclude he was not the dead man.

Until then, he would have a healthy head start.

The heavy crate was loaded into the back of the van. The doors slammed shut. Everything was ready.

"Let's go," he said. The three of them climbed into the van.

Buddy T. smiled as he pulled out of the garage.

He was about to become a martyr to the cause.

Under Undercover

"Why do I have to be a homeless person? Why not Uly or Felix?" Eben asked.

"Because I need them to be available for other things," Boone patiently explained–again. "And also they're a little too . . . noticeable."

"I do not know how to do this," Eben said. "Never, in all my years at the Institute, have I gone undercover as a homeless person. I tell you what! You should bring Ziv. He has been sitting in that car for almost forty-eight hours straight. I am certain he would fit your needed profile. The man is getting scary looking," Eben said.

"He'll be watching Malak. And most homeless people aren't scary," Boone said. "They're just . . . they just don't have anyplace to go."

Eben shook his head. They were two blocks off Grant Park, standing in the northeast corner on the third floor of a parking garage. Boone had already briefed Felix and Uly, who were stationed at the elevators at either end. Both of them making

sure no one stumbled upon their little impromptu briefing.
X-Ray had given Boone a little electronic gizmo designed
to prevent anyone from listening to them with a parabolic
microphone or other device. Plus Croc was there, curled at
Boone's feet. Boone knew the dog would hear or smell an
intruder well before Felix or Uly noticed anything.

It was still dark. They had only a few hours to get
everything in place. So far the plan was for Eben, Callaghan,
and Vanessa to portray members of the homeless population
that were normally found wandering through Grant Park. In
order to look the part, they were sorting through a pile of
clothing of very uncertain origin. It was shoved into a battered
shopping cart Vanessa had secured somewhere. Eben picked
up every item by the barest margin possible. He held out a
green- and yellow-checked shirt, pinched between his thumb
and forefinger as if he were afraid to touch it. It had a large
red stain on the left front pocket and a copper-colored splotch
on the back.

"How?" Eben said. "Someone tell me *how* I am supposed
to wear something like this? What are these stains? So
disgusting." He let the shirt fall back into the basket.

"I sent Uly and Felix shopping at a Goodwill store,"
Vanessa said. "But don't worry. I washed everything at a
laundromat. Then I got it dirty again. It's clean dirt."

"You spent money to wash these clothes? At this time of
night?" Eben asked, skeptical.

"No. Earlier. Boone figured we might need to go under,
told me to gear up," she said. Vanessa was an old hand at
this. She'd found a pair of dirty, dilapidated, and mismatched

canvas tennis shoes. Her bare toe stuck through a hole in the blue one, while the other foot had on a sock that might have been white cotton at some point in its life. She wore a faded pink housedress that came to her knees and a dirty green down jacket with a few of the feathers poking through the fabric.

Eben examined her.

"It's only September. Still warm and humid outside. Won't you stand out in such a thick jacket?" Eben asked.

"That's exactly the point," Callaghan said. "I was undercover at President's Park across from the White House for over a year. Homeless people have to carry or wear whatever they own, regardless of the time of year. She won't stand out at all."

Callaghan pulled a plastic bag full of dark powder from his pocket and opened a bottle of water. Pouring a small pile of the powder into his hand he splashed water on it. Then he rubbed his hands together, making a paste.

"I smell coffee," Eben said.

"Yep. Coffee grounds with a little water mixed in, then rubbed into your face, makes you look really dirty. The paste works its way into the lines and wrinkles of your face. You'll look like you've showered in soil. Everyone will give you a wide berth." Callaghan held out his hand and Vanessa dipped her fingers into the mixture. After rubbing it around her face and neck, and shoving it under her fingernails, she pulled on a yellow winter hat. She was now completely transformed.

Callaghan held out his handful of goo to Eben.

"No," Eben said.

"It's not that bad. You like coffee, don't you?" Callaghan

asked him.

"Yes. But not on my face," he replied.

"You'll get used to it," Callaghan said. Eben sighed and dipped his fingers into the paste and rubbed it over his forehead, cheeks, and chin. Vanessa produced a tube of hair cream and he drizzled some of that into his dark hair. It had the effect of making it look greasy and unwashed. Eben donned the ugly, stained shirt and pulled a long trench coat from the shopping cart. He groaned in disgust as he dressed. A pair of black, battered high-top sneakers with no laces completed the look.

"I cannot believe I'm putting my feet inside these shoes," he said.

"You look like you haven't had a bath in weeks," Boone said, satisfied.

"I will *need* to bathe for weeks once we are done," Eben complained.

"All right, let's do a comm check," Boone said. He put his finger to his ear.

"X-Ray, do you have us?" Boone said.

"Reading all of you five by five," X-Ray replied through the earpiece in Boone's ear. "The signal is perfect."

They all wore specially designed earbuds. Each one was small enough to sit inside their ear canals. For Vanessa, Eben, and Callaghan it was critical that they show nothing. No cords or a Bluetooth or any type of transmitter could be noticeable or their covers would be blown.

One by one they checked off with X-Ray. Once again Boone had to marvel at the relentless march of technology.

These devices were made of transparent plastic. It would be nearly impossible to spot them unless one was looking directly into their ears.

"Okay, I think we're ready," Boone said. Felix and Uly left their posts at the elevators and joined the group.

"One more thing," Callaghan said. He removed a torn and faded yellow scarf, a yellow rubber bracelet, and a folded, dirty baseball cap that was also yellow from his coat pocket.

"I checked with a buddy of mine at Chicago PD. I trust him completely. We each need to wear something yellow. It's today's color of the day. If you've got anything yellow clearly visible on your clothing or body, the cops won't hassle you too much because they'll think you're undercover. If something starts to go south, if we need some kind of diversion, I'm going to start an altercation with a Chicago cop. If someone approaches Malak, even if it's not Buddy, and you want Uly to get them out of there without being noticed, give me a holler on the comm. I'll make a big ruckus. If necessary, I'll get myself taken down and arrested. I'll use my badge to get out of it later."

"Good plan, Pat," Boone said. "For some reason, I don't think Buddy T. is going to show, but I'm going to have Felix on the roof of one of the hotels nearby with the rifle. Uly will be in the crowd, close to Malak. Just in case. And watch out for Ziv. He'll be watching her but we won't see him unless he wants us to. So don't shoot him by accident," Boone said.

"I have a question," Uly said, raising his hand as if he was in grade school. "Yes?" Boone asked.

"How come Felix always gets to be the sniper way up high,

where it's safe? I always have to be down on the ground, close to where all the shooting, stabbing, and exploding happens. X-Ray made me put a tracker on the Tahoe the other day and my face was about six inches from a gazillion pounds of C-4. How come Felix is always the one who gets to shoot?"

"It's simple, really," Felix said, as he removed a sniper rifle from the back of the new Range Rover. He put the stock of the rifle against his shoulder and sighted down the barrel. "I'm a better shot than you are."

"You wish," Uly said.

"Higher scores at Marine Scout Sniper School, my man. The paper don't lie," Felix gloated.

"That's a . . . that's not even . . . I . . ." Uly stammered, annoyed at Felix giving him the needle.

Boone let it go on for a little bit. He knew this back-and-forth banter was a way that teams like this relieved stress before they undertook their mission.

"Uly," Boone said, "Felix is yanking your chain. The truth is, Felix did grade out a little higher than you in sniper training. Barely. But you came out ahead in hand-to-hand combat. Also barely. That's why I need you in the crowd, watching Malak's back. We don't know what we're dealing with. If somebody tries to take her out, I'm going to need both of you."

Uly smiled and flexed his muscles in Felix's direction. Felix smirked and rolled his eyes before he quickly disassembled the rifle. In a few moments it was secured in a specially designed backpack. You couldn't exactly walk down a Chicago street carrying a sniper rifle in plain sight.

"I wish we had better intel," Boone said. "We're flying by

the seat of our pants here. Thanks to Malak, we're higher up in the cell than we've ever been. What bothers me is both her previous meetings with the leadership—at Kitty Hawk and San Antonio—were done in quiet, off-the-grid type places. Now they want a very public meeting in a venue that's bound to be full of innocent civilians. I don't like it."

The team was quiet for a moment. No one spoke up.

"All right, Vanessa, you move out first and get into position. The rest of us will follow at staggered intervals. If they have anybody watching, we want it to look like people are arriving at the park naturally," Boone said.

Vanessa pushed the cart toward the elevators. The squeaky wheels echoed off the concrete floors and walls of the parking garage.

"Croc, you go with Eben," Boone said. "Try and keep him out of trouble."

"What? Oh no," Eben said. "It is bad enough the way these horrible clothes make me smell now. To add to my misery I am to be accompanied by the world's smelliest dog? I must refuse."

"He'll make you look more . . . natural," Boone said. "Trust me."

Croc nudged Eben in the back of the leg with his snout and pushed him toward the stairs. Eben left, muttering curses in Hebrew the entire way.

"Hey, Boone, where are you going to be?" Uly asked as he and Felix readied themselves to head out.

"I'll be here and there," Boone answered.

Additions to the List

I had a new item to add to my list of things I didn't like about being a spy. You can be blown up, kidnapped, stuck with a knife, drugged, have guns pointed at you, and get pigeon poop on your hands. But it's also quite possible you can die from boredom. Even in the middle of a crisis, if you didn't pay attention it was hard to keep focus.

Sitting in the intellimobile with Angela and X-Ray staring at grainy surveillance video of really exciting places like bus stops, car-rental counters, hotel lobbies, and especially traffic cams . . . hundreds of different cars on different streets that went on and on and never, never, ever ended. Well, let's just say I was sure watching that could result in premature death by extreme monotony. I tried hard, really I did. It was important. But my mind is just not suited to this kind of work and it makes me restless.

I put my elbows on the console and rubbed my eyes. They were burning from staring at the screen. It made me wonder if you also could perish from burning eyes. Probably.

My hand automatically went into my pocket and my fingers wrapped around a deck of cards. But Angela had developed a sixth sense for when I was getting fidgety. She glared at me. I meekly withdrew my empty hand and waggled my fingers at her. She shook her head and turned back to look at the screens.

"How many more ways can there be to get out of Chicago?" I groused. "We've been at this forever. I think Buddy T. is gone," I said.

"There's hundreds of ways, in addition to just driving out by car or any other vehicle," X-Ray said. "We've covered the airports, bus stations, and train terminals. But we haven't even begun looking at the marinas or private landing strips or–"

I held up my hands in mock surrender.

"Okay, okay, I get it." In truth, I thought we were wasting our time. It seemed like it would be impossible to find someone who knew how to make sure they weren't going to be found. The thing is, it wasn't an easy leap for me to imagine Buddy being involved in planning something bad. The entire time I'd been around him he was overbearing, obnoxious, and a total jerk. But he'd never seemed like he was really evil enough to be involved in a terrorist plot.

"Did you ever imagine Buddy T. could do something like this?" I asked Angela.

She shrugged. "I guess I never really thought about it, but honestly I'd have to say no. He's a tool, but . . . I don't know. All of these terrorists are sort of hiding in plain sight. Leading what looks like a regular life, until they take action. Maybe being such a jerk was part of it. He had us all fooled," she said.

I thought about that for a minute. Now we knew how the ghost cell always seemed to be around wherever Match was. Buddy never seemed like a good guy. But I just didn't see him having the stones to be involved in something bad up close. Which is why I believed he'd already scrammed.

The tedium was more than I could stand and I needed to stretch. If I didn't, there was a better than fifty-fifty chance I would fall asleep. Which would probably lead to Angela tae kwan do-ing me in the back of the head. Fresh air would do me good.

"Where are you going?" Angela asked sharply as I scooted out of my seat.

"Just need a little air. Then I'll come back in and start with all of the bicycle rental places or something," I said.

Angela gave me a dismissive wave and I headed toward the rear door of the van. As I passed by X-Ray, I noticed he wasn't studying video footage like we were. He was looking at photographs. And I recognized them. They were the photos from Miss Ruby's phone. The one I had managed to steal while she was holding me prisoner.

"What are you doing, X-Ray?" I asked, genuinely curious.

"I'm trying to figure out what the ghost cell is up to," he mumbled. "Something is . . . off."

"I don't get why we aren't looking for car bombs. It's what they've used every time so far. Isn't that their signature?" Angela asked.

"Yes, but there's also something to be said for changing things up. Not using a car bomb because that *is* what we're expecting."

X-Ray made a clucking sound and shook his head. "Despite what you see on television and in the movies, it's not that easy to get your hands on that much C-4 or Semtex plastic explosives. It's heavily regulated. They might be able to buy some on the black market but it would be risky. Especially with every federal agency in the country looking for them. And they already used two in D.C. and four more in Kitty Hawk and San Antonio. I think they've got something else planned," he muttered.

"Like what?" Angela asked. She hit a button, pausing her streaming video on the monitor, and swiveled around in her chair so she could look over X-Ray's shoulder.

"I wish I knew," X-Ray said. "There are a lot of images on here. All of them are from different locations and points of view. There are a lot of shots of the skyline from different angles. But mostly it's pictures of the major skyscrapers, the Sears Tower, the John Hancock Center—there are over sixty buildings in Chicago at least five hundred feet tall. If you were able to take down any one of them, it would cause colossal damage."

"What do you think is going to happen, X-Ray?" Angela asked.

"I don't know," he said. He removed his glasses and rubbed his eyes.

"X-Ray," Angela said, "when is the last time you've gotten some sleep?"

He ignored the question.

"In addition to the photos, Miss Ruby's phone also gave me access to her e-mail and Web browser history. She had received a lot of e-mail alerts and researched a number of websites about Chicago weather patterns, specifically wind velocity and direction. It just makes me wonder. . . ."

"Wonder what, X-Ray?" Angela said.

"It's easier to show you," he said. He punched a few keys on his keyboard.

"I programmed a simulation, using climate data that included wind patterns, humidity, precipitation, and every other climate variable I could think of. Once we determined that whoever we're chasing wants Malak in Grant Park, I started running possible scenarios, with that location as . . ."

He stopped and looked at Angela, not finishing his sentence. He ran his fingers over the keyboard again. Up popped a three-dimensional map of the city with several buildings outlined in bright green. There were a lot of squiggly arrows running in the sky over the building images. Grant Park was outlined in bright red.

"What are we looking at?" Angela asked.

"At first I thought the pictures might be potential targets. Either the cell would try to blow them up or destroy them somehow. Take down a Chicago high-rise during a weekday and your casualties would be in the thousands. But it would take a lot of planning and near-perfect execution to do it. These buildings have much stricter security these days. It would require a lot of explosives, which, like I said, are not that easy to get. And–" X-Ray stopped.

"And what?" Angela prodded him. I understood her impatience. X-Ray had a theory. As smart as he was, it was probably a really good theory, and Angela's mom was in real danger. Angela was going to start demanding answers soon.

"I started thinking. What if the building isn't the target? What if it's *where* they launch the attack from?" he asked.

"What kind of attack?" I asked, trying to ignore the ever-so-slight itching sensation that was starting in the palms of my hands.

"It could be anything," X-Ray said. "You could have a shoulder-mounted surface-to-air missile and take down an aircraft. You could have some kind of gas or bio-terror weapon to release in the atmosphere. It would be possible . . ."

X-Ray kept talking but I was no longer listening. Something was tickling the very corner of my memory. It had to do with the Leopard and Malak and the ghost cell, and what X-Ray was saying tied it all up somehow. We now knew it was because of Buddy T. that they kept showing up wherever we did. But I kept thinking about how the whole thing started. Back in Philadelphia, at Independence Hall.

"John Hancock!" I blurted out.

X-Ray stopped mid-sentence to look at me. Angela stared as if I'd lost my mind.

"What about him?" Angela asked.

"He's the guy who signed his name on the Declaration of Independence in really big letters, right?" I asked.

"Yes," Angela said. "According to legend, he did it so King George III wouldn't have to wear his glasses in order to read—"

"I don't need a history lesson right now," I said, interrupting. "It's the John Hancock one."

"Huh? What makes you think that?" Angela scoffed. But X-Ray was staring off into space, and I knew he was considering it.

Now I had the full-on itch.

"Because they want to send a message not just to the country, but to us. And all of this started in Philadelphia, at Independence Hall with us meeting Malak there. Somehow that's when they knew, or at least suspected that Boone and the SOS team were on to them. X-Ray, take out all of the other buildings in your little weather pattern simulation doodad except the Hancock," I said.

X-Ray punched a few keys. The other building outlines disappeared. Only the Hancock Center was left. The wind pattern arrows crossing through the sky above it led directly over Grant Park.

"That's it!" I said, lurching back to my seat. "Pull up every piece of surveillance footage you can find for all the entrances to that building. Starting from the time Buddy disappeared."

I know it took longer, but it seemed like it was only seconds before X-Ray had it up and running on our monitors. It took another hour and a half of us carefully reviewing every bit of film before we discovered what we were looking for. We made sure to take our time so as not to miss anything. Then we found it.

According to the time stamp on the traffic cam, just a little over an hour previously, a truck marked "Citywide Plumbing" pulled up to a side entrance to the skyscraper. Three men got out and opened the rear doors of the van. They removed a large crate using one of those big hand trucks, the kind people use to move refrigerators and other heavy stuff. Pushing it up to the building's entrance, they waited while a security guard looked at a clipboard, checked their IDs, and finally let them inside.

They were all dressed in identical gray overalls with the company logo on the back. Except that one guy wore yellow high-top tennis shoes. X-Ray zeroed in on his face, blowing it up big on the screen. There was no doubt. It was Buddy T.

Fast-forwarding through the footage we saw two guys come back out. The crate was no longer on the dolly. One of them was Buddy T. with his bright-yellow high-tops. The two of them got in the van and drove away.

One of them was still inside.

"X-Ray," Angela said, "you better find Boone."

Leopard Unleashed

Malak was now officially over the edge, ready to start shooting at something, paranoid. She had been out for an early-morning run, getting her head right before she left for Grant Park. However, the fact that someone had been inside the house the last time she left weighed on her mind. That it was someone who managed to sneak by Ziv and Eben was even more troubling. She only knew Eben by reputation, but Mossad agents were some of the best in the world. And she knew it was nearly impossible to get anything past Ziv. Still, someone had gotten inside. How?

Her current theory for an unobserved entry was that the house must have some kind of secret entrance or tunnel from another nearby structure. But try as she might, she could not find it. And every inch of the house had been searched from the attic to the basement.

As she jogged along the street she took several deep breaths. The last three blocks she sprinted the remaining distance. Reaching the front yard she jogged in place, cooling down from her run, but actually observing to see if anyone had been there while she was gone. She saw nothing out of the ordinary.

Malak took several more deep breaths and did a few stretches, giving every appearance of being a regular, ordinary jogger. To anyone observing her she would look like a young professional woman finishing up her morning exercise. Once done, she would go inside and ready herself for the day. Nothing unusual about anything she was doing.

Malak trotted down the concrete walk along the side of the house to the back door. It was unlikely anyone would have attempted to enter through the front. Climbing the back steps to the rear door, she reached into the pocket of her hoodie, gripping the handle of her pistol. Cautiously, she opened the door, gun at the ready, and taking a very long stride, she stepped inside the house.

Standing still, she listened for several moments. It was quiet. She cleared the house room by room. No one was there. But had someone visited again while she was out? She returned to the back door. Earlier that day at the drugstore she had purchased some supplies to help her determine if anyone visited while she was gone.

Malak knelt and took out her smartphone. It had a flashlight app, which she activated. Before leaving she had carefully sprinkled baby powder on the wooden floor just inside the door. Not enough for someone to notice, but a sufficient amount to leave a sign if anyone had entered through the door. Sure enough, she saw the powder had been disturbed. Someone had been here. But why? They had not left an envelope of new instructions. Had they come to kill her, fooling her with the anticipated meeting at Grant Park? Making her think that would be the place the danger would occur? Was it their plan to catch her off guard here and eliminate the Leopard?

Malak stood and took a moment to consider this evidence. Someone visited the house while she was gone. Had they come to kill her? Did they know she would have taken steps to safeguard the house, but come anyway? Was it all just an attempt to unnerve her? But who was it? Number Two? Or perhaps even Number One?

She lowered herself to the floor again. With her light, she studied the footprints impressed in the powder. They were unusual. There was no full print like a tennis shoe or loafer would leave. Instead she saw a U-shaped heel print, then a few inches from the heel came the triangular outline of a pointed-toe print.

They looked like the tracks someone would leave if they were wearing cowboy boots.

Malak sat back on her haunches, her gun still clutched in her hand. Cowboy boots. Granted, they were not an uncommon type of footwear. Lots of people wore them. But so far as she was aware only one person who knew the location of the safe house regularly wore cowboy boots.

Tyrone Boone.

Angela Unleashed

Angela scrambled out of her seat and headed toward the van's rear door.

"What are you doing?" I asked.

"Going to the Hancock building. We've got to stop these creeps," she said.

"Don't you think we should let Boone handle that?" X-Ray asked.

"X-Ray is right," I said. "We should let Boone decide what to do."

"There's no time, Boone has everyone at Grant Park. There's no one else."

"Angela, wait!" I hollered, but by then she was through the door and gone. I had to go after her, but I didn't even know where the Hancock building was. Let alone what we would do once we got there. Ask the terrorists very nicely if they would mind not blowing something up? Just this once? Ask them if they wanted to see some really cool card tricks, stalling them long enough for Felix and Uly to show up and take them out?

"X-Ray, find Boone," I said. "Tell him where we're headed. And, um, can you text or download a map or directions for how to get to the Hancock building to my phone?"

"I can do that," X-Ray said. "But once you step out of the van, you'll be able to see it. It's only a couple of blocks away."

"Oh," I said sheepishly. I needed to brush up on my geography. Apparently I had been too preoccupied by other stuff, like not getting kidnapped again, to notice the humongous skyscraper close by.

I hopped out on the street and shut the van door. A voice behind me said, "What's going on?" It was so close and unexpected it made me leap in the air in surprise. I made a weird, half-screeching *hooolllygaaaaoossshhhh!* sound. It was Boone. Croc was standing next to him. I knew—and from the look on his face, he knew that I knew—that he had just *poofed* there.

"Why do you keep doing that?" I said, trying to get my frazzled nerves to defrazzle.

"X-Ray called. What's going on? Where's Angela?"

"She took off for the Hancock building. That's the target," I said. As quickly as I could, I filled him in on what we had figured out.

"That's good work," Boone said. He stroked his beard thoughtfully for a second.

"Aren't you going to send everyone there? Evacuate the building? Call the police or something?" I asked. I glanced around. It was early. Checking the time on my phone, I saw it was 5:45 a.m. The streets were starting to come to life with early risers who were heading into work.

Boone shook his head.

"You might be right about the building. Having seen Buddy T. there, you probably are. But they also might be using it as a distraction. Or they might be playing us. They've been a step ahead of us the whole time. Maybe the building is a feint. You saw them take a crate inside and only two guys came out. But the crate might be full of sawdust. Maybe that guy changed clothes and disappeared through a side door to throw us off the trail. They could be trying to draw us there, so we pull everyone off Malak and they take her out. I can't take that chance. I've got to keep the rest of the team on Malak. She's our only link to the top leadership of the cell."

Luckily the Hancock building was not too far away. He pointed over my shoulder and I turned around and there it was. It was huge and tapered at the top with two large antenna-like towers stretching from the roof into the sky. It was hard to miss. But somehow I had still failed to notice it, even though it was so close by.

"Croc, go find Angela," Boone said.

Croc loped around the side of the intellimobile. From where I was standing, I could see past the front of the van down the street to the corner of Michigan Avenue. Seconds passed and I waited for Croc to reappear, but he never did. I knew that he had *poofed.*

"You head for the building and try to find Angela. Wait until I get there," Boone said.

"Where are you going?" I asked.

"I'll be right behind you," he said. "I've got to fill Pat in so he can run the op at the Park. Just in case it's a double cross.

Something is very wrong here."

"Can't you just have X-Ray tell him?"

Boone shook his head. "Malak's life is in danger. I've got to make it clear to him he's in charge now. Face to face. And Ziv might be right. If they know about me, our communications might be compromised."

I knew Boone would get there a lot faster than me, even if he did have to go back and find Agent Callaghan to fill him in. I started down the street at a run but then stopped, remembering something I wanted to tell Boone. I was sure he remembered. But if I'd learned anything these past few days it's don't take anything for granted.

"Hey, Boone!" I called out, turning around. But he was already gone. Out of sight. I sighed and resumed running toward the Hancock building.

I wanted to remind Boone that today was September 11.

Up on the Roof

Grant Park was filling up with eager concertgoers. It was nearing 8:00 a.m. Only half an hour left until the show started. All of the local Chicago television stations had their trucks parked nearby, their satellite antennae reaching into the sky. Cameras were everywhere. An early-morning concert would allow news stations to broadcast coverage all day long. It would help promote the relief effort. It would also be streamed live over the Internet.

Malak moved carefully through the crowd. As always, she wore large sunglasses and kept the hood of her sweatshirt pulled up to cover as much of her face as possible. Her instructions had been to be at the fountain at 8:30 a.m. The Leopard would not take her position without making a thorough reconnaissance of the area first.

She passed by a handful of Chicago cops. They stood listening attentively while a patrol sergeant gave them a security briefing. One of them made brief eye contact with her. Ziv. His disguise was so authentic that even the other officers did not realize he was an imposter.

Malak was constantly amazed at Ziv's ability to blend into his surroundings. Some type of law enforcement disguise was always his first choice. People responded to authority whether it was real or pretend. No matter what city they were in, he always managed to acquire a regulation police uniform. Being dressed as a police officer got you into and out of lots of places with no questions asked. She had no idea how he did it, and that was probably best.

Yet no matter where they were or what their objective was, Ziv managed to do exactly whatever needed to be done. Whether it was impersonating a cop, a Border Patrol agent, or a U.S. Marshal, Ziv always managed to be in the right place at the right time.

Not far away, on a park bench, she spotted Eben. Malak almost had to stifle a laugh. He was possibly the worst undercover homeless person she had ever seen. Though he looked perfectly destitute and dirty, his mannerisms were all wrong. He was nervous and jerky, making eye contact with everyone who passed his way. Still, she was glad he was there. Eben Lavi had tracked her around the globe and nearly caught her. Indeed he had come closer to capturing the Leopard than anyone else ever had. He was not likely to lose his head in a crisis.

She had yet to spot Callaghan and doubted she would. He was too good. But there was no doubt in her mind that he was watching her. And if she were Boone she would have at least one, if not two, sniper on the rooftops nearby. Using her Secret Service training, with her head still facing forward, her eyes moved upward as she scanned the rooftops. She saw no one. No light reflected on a scope. There was no rifle barrel visible. A well-trained sniper always shot from cover. No one ever saw a rifle barrel or a reflection. Boone's people were good.

Slowly and deliberately Malak meandered along. The crowd was growing by the minute. The stage had been set up on the southeast side of the park. There were roadies scurrying about, moving speakers and microphones into place. She stalked through the masses circling toward the fountain. Another glance at her watch. It was 8:10 a.m. Twenty minutes until the meeting.

All morning Malak had considered the cowboy boot footprints she had found in the safe house. The prints in and of themselves did not prove it was Boone who had entered there. But on the list of suspects, he had to be near the top. He knew the location. But try as she might she could not believe Boone was the intruder.

In her years as the Leopard, Malak had honed her survival instincts to a keen edge. Making snap judgments about people was often the difference between life and death. It was hard for her to believe that Boone was spying on her. Or was he? Could Boone somehow think Malak had been turned? That now she was giving the ghost cell the inside information on the location of his team? It couldn't be true. Being undercover for so long, being in the game for this many years, made you paranoid and suspicious of everyone. It just couldn't have been Boone.

But then, the caller on the phone had asked her specifically

if she knew him. Why? They had the safe house under
surveillance. Did they observe him entering it and looking for
her? Is that why they asked her if she was connected to him
in some way?

Impossible–Boone would not be foolish enough to come
to the safe house. He was too smart. He wouldn't take the
chance. Except.

Except for one nagging thing she could not reconcile or
explain away.

After the raid at Kitty Hawk, she had been flown to
Number Three's ranch in Texas in a private aircraft. It was
a massive, sprawling spread in the middle of nowhere. After
meeting with Number Three, she waited in a small guesthouse
near the landing strip until the plane arrived to fly her to
Chicago. Boone and his dog, Croc, had suddenly and without
warning visited her in the guesthouse. There he had briefed
her on the current status of their situation and informed her
that Angela and Q were both safe.

At first she had been grateful to Boone. He had taken a
great risk to find her. He could have been caught or captured
by any of Number Three's security guards. And after seeing
the boot prints, that fact began to nag at her. He *hadn't* been
seen or caught.

How had Boone avoided Number Three's security? With
an old dog in tow?

Malak closed her eyes and recalled the memory. She had
just come out of the guesthouse bathroom and Boone was
sitting in a chair. Croc was stretched out on the couch like
he owned it. Boone claimed his tech genius had given him a

small gizmo that scrambled or otherwise allowed him to avoid the camera surveillance. It was possible, she supposed. Boone had amazing gadgets at his disposal. But he still would have had to cross several hundred yards of open ground to reach the guesthouse. That seemed like an insurmountable obstacle for even the most fabulous technology.

It was like he had appeared out of thin air.

Now she wondered. What if his tech had failed? What if the device hadn't scrambled the cameras and the ghost cell saw him inside the house? They would automatically be suspicious. Maybe that explained their interest in Boone.

Malak had been so worried about Angela that she hadn't given Boone's sudden appearance in Texas the careful consideration it deserved. He had proven himself loyal and capable during the raid at Kitty Hawk. But now . . . too many questions.

Her watch said 8:15 a.m. She needed to clear her mind of these extraneous thoughts. The Leopard must be ready to strike. Drawing several deep, cleansing breaths, she refocused on the task at hand. It was time for her to take her position at the fountain. Cutting through the gathering throng, she headed to the spot where she had been instructed to wait.

There would be time to worry about Tyrone Boone later.

Getting In

I found Angela and Croc near the main entrance of the
Hancock building. I was out of breath. A "few blocks away"
in Chicago is a lot farther than it sounds. And finding Angela
and Croc was easy because they looked like they were playing
some sort of weird game.

The game went like this. Angela kept trying to get close to
the entrance of the building. And Croc kept getting in her way
and preventing her doing just that. Angela would step to her
right or her left—back up or step forward—fake right, then go left,
and any other combination of moves she could think of. Nothing
worked. Croc did not want Angela rushing into a potentially
dangerous situation. And Angela was not going to wear Croc
down. Furthermore, Angela was not enjoying the game.
"Knock it off, Croc!" I heard her complain bitterly when I
arrived. "I need to get inside."

"Are you guys playing tag?" I asked, coming to a stop and
trying hard not to show how out of breath I was.

"He's really starting to annoy me," Angela said. Croc sat

back on his haunches; the fact that he was annoying Angela was not bothering him at all.

"So I gathered," I said. "Boone said he would be here in a minute and—"

"We need to get inside and find a way to the roof," Boone said from behind me. I jumped again. I really wished he would quit doing that.

"How are we going to do that?" Angela asked, apparently not noticing he had just appeared out of nowhere. She must have been preoccupied with Croc and thought Boone had arrived with me. This time I noticed that Boone was breathing hard and his face was sweaty.

"I don't know yet," Boone said. "X-Ray downloaded the building plans to my phone. He's trying to crack the building security but it's going to take him time. We need to find a way to the roof."

"Um. Boone?" I asked. "Can't you just go to the roof? I mean like . . . you know . . . how you go places?"

"Not right now. Not yet, at least," he said, his thumb swiping over the screen of his phone as he studied the plans.

"But I don't—" I started to say.

"Can we talk about this later?" Boone said. And he sort of snapped when he said it. Not like Angela does when she's tense or mad at me. But there was a warning tone in his voice. Telling me to change the subject because he didn't want to discuss it right now. Ever since we met Boone I couldn't remember him ever sounding like that.

I knew better than to press it. Angela gave me a wide-eyed look and was chewing on her lip. Which meant she really wanted to speak up but was holding herself back. She'd picked up on Boone's mood too.

The building was starting to fill up with office workers. Once Boone had quickly reviewed the building plans, we went into the lobby. This entrance of the building had a security desk, but instead of turnstiles or metal detectors everyone had to go past the guard station and insert a card into a slot on the elevator to make the doors open.

"Can't you just use one of your fake badges to get us access?" Angela asked.

"Maybe. But not without raising a lot of questions. And if I used a police or Homeland Security badge, I'd have a hard time explaining why I have two teenagers and a dog with me," Boone said.

Then he said, "X-Ray, we need to get on the elevators. Can you help us out?"

At first I thought he was talking to the air, because he wasn't wearing a Bluetooth. We gave him a curious look, and he pointed to his ear. "New tiny two-way earbuds. A new X-Ray toy," he said.

He waited a minute. Then he said. "Okay. I understand. Keep working on the roof."

Boone shook his head. "He's still hacking through the building security to get us up on the roof. We don't have much time. But that appears to be the most likely place for them to strike from. So we need to figure out a way to get up those elevators."

The itch was growing stronger. The concert would begin soon. I envisioned Grant Park filling up with people. And then something really bad happening. I had to do something.

A few seconds later, a large cluster of workers came through the entrance. Most of them had the plastic elevator ID cards pinned to their jacket pockets or blouses. I left Boone and Angela standing in their spot and headed toward the oncoming group.

I pulled a deck of cards out of my pocket and approached a balding, middle-aged guy with a pass hanging from the pocket of his suit coat. He was staring straight ahead, lost in thought, a briefcase in one hand and a paper cup of coffee in the other. The expression on his face said the last thing he wanted was to be bothered.

"Excuse me, mister," I said, stepping in front of him.

"What?" he said, his eyes finally focusing on me.

"I lost my wallet and I need to get enough money for the El to get home. How about I show you a really cool card trick and you can give me a buck or two?" I said.

"What? No . . . get out of my way, I'm late for work," he said, trying to step around me.

"It'll just take a minute," I said, fanning the cards in one hand. "Please, mister, I really need the money."

"No!" he said. "And shouldn't you be in school or something?" He tried to step around me but I put my hand on his arm to slow him.

"Please," I said.

"Let me go!" He jerked his arm away and stepped around me. "I'm reporting you to security."

I hustled back to Angela and Boone.

"What did you just do?" Angela asked.

"A little sleight of hand," I said, holding up the elevator pass I'd lifted off the guy's pocket while his attention was diverted.

"We better hurry, though," I said. "He's going to report me. Once he finds out his pass is missing, they'll probably deactivate it."

When we reached the elevator, I inserted the card in the slot and the doors opened. We all got on. Croc "insisted" on getting on first.

"Where to?" I asked.

"Top floor," Boone said; "we've got to get to the roof." It took a couple minutes for the elevator to reach the top floor. It's a tall building. We arrived at the floor beneath the observation deck. The observation deck had its own special elevator and there was no roof access, according to the floor plans. That was probably to keep people from attempting to do exactly what we were trying to do.

The door opened and Boone glanced down at his phone.

"This way," he said.

We turned left out of the elevator and then left again at the first corridor and followed it to the end. There we found a door with a sign reading, "Roof Access. Emergency Personnel Only. Do Not Open. Alarm Will Sound." The door was barred with a heavy stainless steel touch bar.

"X-Ray, are you–?" Boone began.

Before he could finish his question, there was a loud *click* and the door popped open. X-Ray scared me a little.

Before us was a stairway. At the top of the stairway was another alarmed door, which X-Ray had taken the liberty of already deactivating.

As we reached the top of the stairs, Boone pushed the door all the way open and we stepped out onto the roof of one of the world's tallest buildings.

The first thing you notice when you are on the roof of a skyscraper is the wind. Because at that altitude it is blowing so strongly, it nearly drives you to your knees. The second thing is that a skyscraper roof is a lot bigger and covered with more stuff than you would think.

The surface of the roof was covered with a thin layer of gravel on top of asphalt. The top of the Hancock Center building had an unusual design. As we exited the door, we found that most of the roof surface was taken up by a large steel structure. Like a small pole barn sitting on top of the skyscraper. From the roof of that rectangular structure rose two incredibly large, tall antennas. Off to our right was a whole series of cooling units. Maybe half a dozen of them, whirring away. There was smoke coming out of them. And I could hear water running.

"Is that smoke?" I asked. I was afraid that perhaps a fire had already started in the building and the sprinkler system had activated to extinguish it.

"No, it's steam," Boone said. "Those units circulate water through the building for cooling systems. When the warm water is pumped up to the roof it can give off steam on a humid day like today."

The steam, the water noise, and the wind made the whole scene eerie.

Between the thrum of the machines and the rushing air it

was also really hard to hear.

"Stay close," Boone said. "Don't get too close to the edges. The wind can gust strong enough to blow you right off if you're not careful. We're going to look for anything out of the ord—"

He never got to finish because about two inches to the right of my head, the metal wall behind me was hit by something hard. Several times. A bullet had bitten into the metal surface and bits of shrapnel went flying. I felt them sting the back of my neck. Then a bunch more bullets came chattering along the ground from an automatic weapon. Concrete chips, gravel, and all kinds of fragments went flying everywhere.

"Take cover!" Boone shouted.

He didn't have to say it twice.

The Leopard Waits

Malak went to the appointed spot and sat on the bench by the fountain. Just as she had been instructed. With her left hand she held the phone to her ear. Her right hand remained buried in the pocket of her hoodie, gripping the handle of her pistol. She studied the crowd. Every so often she nodded and repeated words like "yes," "no," "I see," "really?" and "that's true," making it sound like she was holding a conversation. It would have been helpful to actually be talking with Ziv or even Callaghan. But the phone had come to her from the ghost cell. It might be monitored. She could not risk it.

Her eyes moved rapidly behind her glasses. She was at an extreme disadvantage. The voice on the phone had been disguised. Malak had no idea if she was to meet a man or a woman. In her experience, most terror cells tended to be run by men. But she had met Miss Ruby in Texas and Elise had been Number Five. Obviously the ghost cell did not always follow convention.

She shifted nervously in her seat. She looked quickly at

the time. It was 8:32 a.m. It could be that her contact had been delayed. But she doubted it. Ziv had been right. This was a setup. If she had any sense, she should get up and walk away. But she had to wait. To be sure.

Angela appeared in her mind's eye. She was glad her daughter was out of danger. And Q as well. She hoped her concerns about Boone were unfounded. That right now Boone had them under guard at a hotel or other safe location. The thought made her feel good. She had only gotten to know Q a little bit, but she liked the kid. It would be good for her daughter to have a brother like Q. Maybe he would keep her a little more relaxed. A quirky, slightly goofy brother might sand off some of the rough edges of intensity Angela had inherited from her mother.

The throng was pressing in all around her. It appeared as if thousands of people would be enjoying the concert this morning. Her cell phone now read 8:35 a.m. Something had gone wrong. The Leopard needed to concentrate. *Stop thinking about Angela,* she told herself.

A man suddenly stepped out of the crush of people and wormed his way onto the bench next to her, seated to her right. Malak tensed and readied herself to attack, but before she could move the man spoke in a hushed voice. And she noticed his hands were buried in his windbreaker. He no doubt had a gun pointed at her.

"Do not move," he said. "Place the phone on the bench beside you. Very, very slowly remove your other hand from your pocket. I know you are holding a gun, do not even think about attempting to use it."

Malak turned her head to study the man.

"Look straight ahead," he warned her. "Don't glance in my direction."

All she could tell from her peripheral vision was that he was medium height, wearing large sunglasses, a baseball cap and quite possibly a fake beard. Malak was momentarily frozen. Ziv, Callaghan, and everyone watching her would assume she had made contact. The plan had been for them to follow her. Number Two had said they would meet her and go to meet Number One. Then the team would take them both down. But something about this felt off to her. For a reason she couldn't explain, she didn't think this man was Number Two.

"You must be Number Two," she said.

"Do not talk. Do not ask questions," he said.

"Do you know who you are speaking to?" Malak asked, her voice quiet but full of anger.

The man, whoever he was, was well trained. He did not look in her direction.

Nor did he respond to her taunt. At that point she realized something. They had not sent Number Two. The plan might still be to take her to a meeting place. But they had sent someone they felt confident would be able to handle the Leopard if she decided to show her claws.

"When are we leaving to meet Number One?" she asked.

"We are not going anywhere. We will sit here and enjoy the concert. When it is done, I will leave first. Then you will go. You will be contacted with further instructions. This is a test, to make sure you understand to do what you are told," he said.

"That was not the arrangement!" Malak fairly hissed at the man.

"Lower your voice," he said calmly.

Malak stared straight ahead. It was difficult to remain still. Something was wrong. Ziv had been right. They had never intended for her to meet Number One. She feared her cover had been blown.

Because Malak was being watched, she had been unable to take part in a premission briefing. If she had, they would have come up with signals for her to give if she ran into trouble. A series of gestures she could make that would spring the team into action and take down the potential killer sitting next to her.

The music was starting. It was getting loud. She was not wearing a wire. There was no way for them to hear her.

A memory came to her. From the time she served with Pat Callaghan on protection details while they were still with the Secret Service. Whenever one of them had gone undercover, they had created a signal. It looked completely normal, but gave notice that something had gone wrong and the agent was about to take action and backup was required.

"Well," Malak said, "I guess we may as well enjoy the music." As she spoke she stretched her legs out straight in front of her, crossing them at the ankles. She also crossed her arms. It put her in position for her next move.

"Don't make any sudd—" the man started to say.

He never finished whatever he intended to say. Malak pivoted from her waist and drove her elbow into the man's throat. It shattered his hyoid bone and crushed his larynx.

Though the man was unable to breathe, he tried desperately to pull the gun from his pocket. She had counted on this. The smart thing would have been to pull the trigger with the gun still inside the pocket. But the brain's instinct was to draw and then shoot. Malak stood and turned quickly in front of him. If he were able to fire a shot, she would need to use her body to try and keep the bullet from entering the crowd.

But the man, as well trained as he was, was not the Leopard. She grabbed him by the ears and drove her knee into his face. She felt and heard the satisfying crunch of his nose breaking above the sound of the music. People next to her on the bench and others who had gathered near the fountain reacted in horror. Some screamed and moved away from her. But before a full-on panic could set in, Callaghan emerged from the crowd, followed by Uly. Callaghan held up a badge. "FBI!" he shouted, using one of the vast array of IDs he had his disposal.

"You got the signal," she whispered to him, her body relaxing as the adrenaline rush subsided.

"Yeah. I got it. Now get out of here. But don't go back to the safe house. Ziv is waiting at the park's northeast entrance. He's got a police cruiser. He'll get you somewhere safe."

"What's going on, Pat? Is Angela okay?" Malak asked.

"I don't know what's going on. Angela is with Boone. We've got to assume your cover is blown. Get out of here. Now."

She didn't wait. Uly picked the guy up by the collar and deftly handcuffed him and disappeared into the crowd, dragging the semiconscious, choking man along. Malak pulled her hoodie up over her head. Clutching her pistol inside her pocket, she moved quickly through the mass of people toward the waiting Ziv.

All along the way, she thought about what Callaghan had said regarding Angela. He had said she was with Boone.

But he didn't say she was safe.

No Place to Hide

"Take cover, take cover!" Boone shouted again. He and Croc broke to the left and Angela and I went right, looking for something–anything–to hide behind. And we discovered to our immediate horror that there aren't a whole lot of safe places to hide on a skyscraper roof. Especially when you are trying to get away from someone with an automatic weapon. There were all kinds of vents and pipes and stuff but nothing that would protect us from the bullets. Except–the cooling units.

It had to be the guy Buddy left behind who was shooting. Unless there were already more terrorists inside the building we weren't aware of. Which was entirely possible. If they wanted to blow up a building they would probably need more than one guy. What if there were more guys with guns headed up the stairs now? We'd walked into an ambush!

"Over here!" Boone hollered, drawing the gunman's fire away from our position.

"This way!" Angela shouted. We sprinted at an angle

toward one of the air-conditioning units and dove behind it just as the shooter returned his attention to us. A spray of bullets ricocheted off the metal side of the air conditioner.

Here is another thing I have learned about being shot at. In the movies or TV they make it look like the hero has these superhuman reflexes. He always knows exactly where the shooter or shooters are located. The hero turns and fires his weapon, making a miraculous shot, and takes the bad guys out.

This is a big fat fake.

First of all, when you're in a noisy environment like the top of a skyscraper, you can barely hear the shots over the wind noise. Sometimes automatic weapons use sound suppressors, and there's just this little *piff, piff, piff* sound. So it's not until bullets strike the ground or the wall near you that you even realize you're being shot at. The bullets are flying and a shooter who knows what he's doing is constantly on the move. All you can do is try to make yourself as small as possible and hope that he is a horrible shot. The trouble with that plan is that an automatic weapon holds a lot of ammo, so he doesn't have to be a great shot. He can spray bullets everywhere until he hits something. You need to be lucky or you need someone to take him out.

"Do you see him?" Angela shouted.

I didn't say anything.

"Q! Do you see him?" Angela shouted at me, which only served to bring what sounded like another several dozen bullets blasting in our direction. The gun made that *piff, piff* sound and the rounds ricocheted off the metal in front of us.

"No," I said, "he's shooting from over there somewhere."
I nodded with my head.

"That's helpful," she said. We were squatting on the
ground, our backs pressed against the air conditioner.

"If you don't peek out from your hiding place to look for
the shooter, you don't get shot," I said.

"Where's Boone?" she asked, ignoring my explanation of
how to survive being shot at.

"He went in the other direction," I answered.

To make matters even worse, the wind picked up and now
it was roaring across the roof.

"You're *really* not being helpful!" she yelled over the wind.

"My level of helpfulness decreases dramatically when I'm
being shot at!" I yelled back.

I never ceased to marvel at Angela. If it came down to
it, I bet she could probably pass the test to become a Secret
Service agent right now. Here we were, on top of one of the
world's tallest buildings, pinned down by a gunman. Said
gunman was likely going to set off a bomb or something in
the next few minutes. And Angela was approaching the entire
scenario like it was an algebra problem: find "x," "x" being
the crazed shooter with a machine gun. I'll stick to magic,
thank you very much.

We heard Croc bark and Boone shout "Over here!"
again, his voice barely carrying over the sound of the rushing
wind. That was followed immediately by a blast of automatic-
weapons fire. Boone was still trying to draw the shooter's
attention away from us. Which made me think about Boone
and why he didn't just *poof* behind the guy and knock him out

or something. Then I remembered how he'd looked so tired and sweaty down on the street. Maybe he was sick. Maybe you couldn't *poof* as well when you were ill.

"We've got to move," Angela said. "We need to split up. It will help Boone or Croc get close enough to take him down. If we stay here he'll get us both eventually."

I didn't like the sound of him "getting us both eventually" at all. But I liked the idea of running to another location even less. So far this one had stopped all the bullets. It seemed perfectly safe to me.

"I'll head toward the structure. You run along behind these air conditioners to the other end. If you spot Boone, try to get his attention. Maybe he can take the guy out."

Angela didn't wait for my agreement. She raised herself to a crouch and ran back toward the steel structure. I wanted to follow after her. Instead I ran along behind the air conditioners, keeping them between the shooter and me. I think it's probably the fastest I've ever run in my life. And then I ran faster because a trail of bullets started following me. I skidded to a stop at the last air conditioner. I didn't see Angela anywhere. For a moment I thought I saw a flash of orange on the roof of the steel building but I wasn't sure.

My eye caught movement to my left and I saw Angela peek around the corner of the steel edifice. She must have circled all the way around looking for the gunman. I pointed up to the roof and she shook her head. She hadn't seen the shooter.

I looked everywhere for any sign of Boone or Croc. Nothing. And right then I got hit hard with *the itch*. Only this time it was different. My stomach lurched and I felt a little nauseated and dizzy. And when I glanced back at Angela, I saw she had one of those red laser-targeting dots in the center of her forehead.

I didn't even think. "Angela!" I cried.

The next thing I knew, I had pushed Angela to the ground. A bullet struck the concrete right where she had been standing. Shrapnel flew everywhere.

I'm sometimes a little klutzy and I had launched myself at her awkwardly. My momentum spun me around and I felt something punch me hard in the thigh. I also felt sick to my stomach, like I wanted to throw up.

The next thing I saw was a guy landing on the roof in a clumsy heap next to us. He was wearing one of those orange hazmat suits. The kind they use when someone has to clean up chemical spills or doesn't want to be infected by a zombie virus. A small machine pistol landed next to him. He scrambled to his hands and knees and was about to rise up. But Croc had other plans.

At first I thought he jumped. But I don't know if he actually leaped from the top of the structure or just *poofed* from somewhere. I was fighting a severe case of nausea and my vision was a little blurry. Either way, he landed right on the guy's back. Croc's weight drove him hard into the roof surface and shattered his glass faceplate. We heard a loud *ooof* through the broken helmet. Croc went on the attack, snarling, barking, and growling and in a few seconds the guy's hazmat suit was torn to pieces. Whoever designs those things should probably hope there is never a zombie virus that affects dogs. They're going to need better suits.

The guy finally made it to his feet and tried kicking at Croc. The terrorist had no idea this was an exercise in futility. Croc was everywhere and nowhere at once. It quickly reached the point where it's almost futile to describe how it looked. There just isn't anything to compare it to that doesn't sound ridiculous or like you're having a hallucination. Croc appeared and reappeared all over and around the guy. Each snap of Croc's jaws drove the guy back toward the edge of the roof. Somehow he recovered enough to reach inside the shredded suit and draw a big knife.

Big mistake, as this only made Croc madder. The guy swung the knife in a vicious arc and Croc dodged it easily. Well, not dodged—he just disappeared. I'm sure the guy couldn't believe what he was seeing. Before the attacker could recover for another swipe, Croc rematerialized in the air and bit down hard on the knife-wielding arm. Now the man screamed in real agony. As Croc landed on his paws, arm still clamped in mouth, he pulled the guy around in a semicircle. Then he let go. The guy tried to recover. He didn't realize how Croc had herded him. Croc had used the man's momentum to drive him right to the roof's edge. The wind, his wounded body, and the fact that he was off balance were big disadvantages. For a second he teetered on the edge of the roof. With a scream I'll never forget, he tumbled over the side.

I was stunned. In shock, I think, because my stomach hurt and I still wasn't sure what had happened to me. Despite how yucky I felt, seeing all these people die in front of me these last few days was bothering me. Yes, the guy was a bad man.

A killer. Not only a killer, but also a fanatic. A terrorist, who would have wiped out all of us without a second thought. Still, watching someone plunge to their death didn't make me feel heroic or happy or even relieved. For a few brief seconds I felt incredibly sad. I couldn't comprehend how some people could hate other people so much. That guy who just died must have had a family. People he cared about and loved just like I did. Before he started shooting at me I didn't wish him any ill at all.

But then I thought about the fact that I was alive and he wasn't and another part of me was glad about that. Mostly I wanted to curl up in a ball right then and not think about any of this. But I knew I couldn't.

Angela shook me out of my reverie.

"Q, I know you just saved my life and all," she said, "but what the heck did you just do?"

"What do you mean?" I rolled over onto my back. I felt like I'd been run over.

Angela bounded to her feet and I managed to stand, groaning with every movement. A wave of dizziness hit me and I wobbled and Angela caught hold of my arm to steady me.

"Q? Are you all right?" she asked.

"I feel sick," I said. And then I was. I puked right there on top of the Hancock building. I put my hands on my knees, trying to take in air.

"There aren't any more people who are going to shoot at us up here, are there?" I asked.

"I don't think so," she said.

"Good. Because I don't think I can move."

"Q? What just happened? You moved across the roof really fast."

"No, I didn't. I couldn't have. It's not possible," I said.

"Q, come on. You were at least twenty yards away and you crossed the distance almost faster than I could see. You saved my life." She was still holding on to my arm.

I felt so horrible I didn't want to think about it. Something *had* happened. But I couldn't wrap my mind around it. And my head hurt too much to do any heavy thinking.

"If I saved your life, we're even," I said. "But it was mostly Croc." We looked over at Boone's old dog, now lying on the roof, resting, his head up, tongue out, panting away, looking at us like nothing unusual had happened at all.

"Q!" Angela said. "You're shot!" She was pointing to a hole in my cargo shorts where a bullet had entered. I remembered feeling like something had punched me in the thigh when I tackled her.

"I don't feel shot," I said, reaching inside my pocket and removing some of my stuff. Out of sheer luck, the bullet had hit one of my magic coins, which had been lying directly over the top of a deck of cards. It had punctured the coin, but the cards had stopped it from doing any serious damage.

I held up the ruined deck with a bullet wedged in it and waggled my fingers.

"Told you they were magic," I said.

This time Angela actually bent her head and put her forehead in the palm of her hand before she groaned. "You're hopeless."

"Where's Boone?" I asked, suddenly realizing he was nowhere to be seen.

"Up here," came his familiar voice. He was standing on top of the structure in the center of the roof.

"We've got a problem," he said, "a huge problem."

The Big Problem

We had to climb a ladder to reach him on top of the power plant. It's not really fun to do when you feel like barfing again at any minute. There was something he wanted us to see. Boone was talking to X-Ray on his little fancy earbud thing. He was standing next to three shiny metal tubes that looked sort of like cannons. They were next to the base of one of the antennas and pointed directly toward the center of downtown Chicago. On top of each tube were two glass canisters with plastic hoses leading to the ends of the cannons. Each canister held a different color of liquid.

"What the heck are those things?" Angela asked.

"Some type of chemical weapon," Boone said.

"Uh. Boone?" I asked.

"Yes?"

"They aren't going to go off or anything, are they?" I was having a pretty traumatic day so far. Chemical weapons exploding in my vicinity might just send me over the edge.

Boone held up a black plastic case that had some frozen

red LED numbers on its glass face.

"Nah," he said. "I pulled the timer. X-Ray has J.R. sending a team here to secure these tanks, then–" Boone was interrupted by the sounds of screams. At first it was hard to tell exactly what was happening. But all of sudden we heard horns honking and people shouting. All the way up here on the top of the building we could hear noise and confusion coming from the streets below.

"X-Ray what is–" Boone stopped talking and the color drained from his face.

"Boone," Angela and I said at the same time.

"X-Ray? X-Ray? Can you hear me?" Boone said. He was quiet a moment as if he was listening. Then he tapped his ear a couple of times. He removed the little earbud transmitter and looked at it. "Looks like communications have gone offline."

"What's wrong?" Angela said.

Boone was silent for several moments.

"Before I lost him, X-Ray said reports are just coming in over various news outlets," he said. His voice was shaking. "There have been chemical weapons attacks in Atlanta, Paris, and Los Angeles. Antiterrorism squads in New York and London foiled the attacks there. Details are sketchy but it appears that the attacks were launched at 8:46 a.m. First responders are being deployed, air traffic is grounded, the military is on high alert, and evacuation plans for each city are in place, but this is bad."

I looked at my phone. It was almost 9:00 a.m.

"Why 8:46 a.m.?" Angela asked. I knew the answer. I was only a kid when it happened but we'd studied it in school.

"That's when the first plane hit the World Trade Center on 9/11," I said.

None of us knew what to say. What we'd just managed to do, stopping an attack in Chicago, didn't feel as satisfying anymore. No matter how many times my brain tried to tell me it could have been worse. It was bad enough.

"We've got to get moving," Boone finally said. "Croc, take this timer to X-Ray. Let him look it over. Maybe he can trace the components somehow, give us a lead." Croc took the instrument in his mouth and disappeared.

Neither Angela nor I were surprised by Croc's disappearance, but no matter how many times you see it, it's still startling. I guessed now was not the time to ask questions. Boone took out his phone and looked at it. Apparently it wasn't working either. We both checked our phones. No service.

"Okay, I can't raise anyone. I've got to get to the park and find out what happened with Malak," he said. "I need the two of you to get back to the intellimobile. Wait there until you hear from me. Your parents are at the park. Art and Marie will make sure they're safe. I'll tell them you're safe. But listen. Go straight to the van. You should get there before your parents get back to the hotel. The streets are going to be chaos. I'll tell them X-Ray is one of my roadies and you were waiting with him to be ready to evacuate at a moment's notice. You'll be safe with X-Ray. And as soon as I can, I'll send Croc back to you. X-Ray has some skills besides tech and . . . if anything else happens . . . he can . . . he'll know what to do. Now go. They're evacuating the building by now. I'm sure they're using the elevators to get as many people out as quickly as possible, but if not you'll have to take the stairs. So just blend into the crowd and get out as fast as you can. Head for the van the minute you reach the street."

"Boone, we got here in time, what happened?" Angela asked. "If this is the ghost cell, they've been shadowing us the whole time. If they've been focused on taking out the SOS team, why would they hit all these other places? It doesn't make sense."

"It's starting to. I'm thinking this was part of the plan all along. They played us. The cell made us close in and circle our wagons, thinking our team or the city we were going to was the next target. Then they waited until we arrived in the biggest city on the tour. I think it was the plan all along. It made me look inward too closely, and it gave them the perfect opportunity to go big. I messed up. I messed up bad."

"Boone. You can't honestly think this is your fault?" I asked.

Boone just shrugged. But the expression on his face right then was like someone who had done a thing that was so horrible, they would never forgive themselves.

"Take the stairs from the roof and get back to the elevators. I've got to go," he said.

Angela and I were still in shock. We didn't know what else to do so we shuffled our way to the stairway door. When we reached it, I wanted to ask Boone something.

"Hey, Boone," I said, turning around.

But he was already gone.

Getting Out

We retraced our steps down the stairs and to the bank of elevators. As we walked, people were pouring out of the offices on the top floor. Everyone was trying to get out at once and the nervousness and tension were palpable. There were several security guys in blue blazers with tablets standing by each elevator. They were checking people off as they went by. The building's security staff must have had a list of their tenants' employees as part of their evacuation plan.

There was a crush of people at the elevators. Angela and I tried to get in line and wait for the next available car. The security guys were taking names as people stepped into the cars. They had a system for making sure everyone registered in the building got out. We weren't registered. Another elevator car arrived and we tried to get on.

"Name?" the blue-coated guy asked.

"Tucker and Munoz," Angela said without missing a beat.

"Is that one name or two names? Tucker Anne Munoz?" he asked, his brow knitted as he scanned a list of names on his tablet.

"It's our last names," Angela said. "Tucker *and* Munoz."

The security guy hadn't been paying attention but now he looked at us. And he got a confused look on his face. "Company?" he asked.

"We're here on a school project. We were interviewing people at the Advantage Automated Graphics offices for our school paper," Angela said. "Do you know what's going on? We're really scared." She put her arm around my shoulders. "My stepbrother has social anxiety disorder. He's freaking out a little. I need to get him out of here," she said. "It's okay, Q. It's going to be okay." She squeezed my shoulder as she looked at me with the moony, sad eyes again.

I gave her a dirty look at first, but then tried to look scared and socially anxious. We couldn't afford any questions. Questions would lead to us being up on the roof where there were three canisters of liquid poison. And that would be hard for us to explain.

Right then another elevator door opened and six guys in black jumpsuits with large duffel bags walked out. Dollars to doughnuts it was J.R.'s clean-up crew. That J.R. doesn't mess around.

The guys flashed credentials at the security guy and headed down the hallway that would eventually lead them to the roof stairway. While the guard was watching them, Angela pulled me into the car and pushed the button.

"Hey!" the guard shouted. "What did you say—"

"Sorry," Angela yelled as the door was closing, "I need to get him out of here or he'll have a total meltdown."

The door shut before he could do anything.

"Social anxiety disorder?" Our ears were popping as the elevator descended.

"Stop complaining about plans that work," she said.

"What is Advantage Automated Graphics?" I asked.

"I memorized some of the company names on the doors as we passed by the first time. In case we got caught we were going to need some kind of excuse."

"Okay, but next time could I have something besides social anxiety disorder?"

"Like what?" she asked, not really paying attention to me.

"I don't know. A disease where loud noises turn me into a ninja or something," I said.

"You're hopeless."

I had no argument. I was starting to feel like a human being again.

The elevator door opened. It was like stepping into a Hollywood disaster movie. The lobby was a sea of running, screaming people. Crowds surged out of the other elevator cars like a flash flood shooting out of a canyon. The building security force was overwhelmed. Announcements over the intercom asking for calm had no effect. Everyone was running for their lives. The main doors leading out through the lobby were jammed by waves and waves of people.

"You get in front," Angela said. "You're taller and can see over the crowd. Let's try to stick close to the wall. There will be fewer people on the edges. Should be easier to reach the doors."

Angela wanted to be a Secret Service agent. I was willing

to bet she had already studied the Secret Service training manual. She'd probably already memorized the "How to Evacuate a Building During an Emergency" chapter. Since I didn't have a better suggestion I stepped into the crowd.

When I was growing up in California, my mom often took me to the beach. Sometimes the waves would be really rough. Even if you only went into the water up to your knees, the surf rolled in hard and could drive you into the sand. Being swept up by the crowd felt worse. Everyone was in an absolute panic to get out. Angela grabbed my belt and held on as I tried to plow my way through the river of terrified humanity.

In front of me a woman fell down and I stopped to help her to her feet.

"People are out of control," Angela shouted into my ear over the noise. "We need to find another way out of here."

"How?" I said. "We can barely move as it is."

We cleared the little hallway from the bank of elevators and entered the main lobby. There was a large semicircular wooden desk where the security guys sat. It was deserted. I darted behind it and Angela followed me as we watched the rest of the crowd keep pressing toward the front doors. Unable to contain the mass of human beings trying to fit through, the glass in the front doors and the windows next to the doors shattered. People started flooding through the smashed windows ignoring the broken glass.

"What are we going to do?" Angela asked.

"I don't know. But I think we have to get back to the van as fast as we can. If my mom and Roger find out we aren't where they think we are . . ." I let the words trail off. If they learned we were running around the streets of Chicago during a national emergency, we were toast. I suspected Marie, Art, and Boone would be hustling Roger and Mom back to the hotel as quickly as they could. The first thing they would want to do is find us.

As it turned out, Boone didn't let us down.

I heard a bark behind me and looked around. There sat Croc on his haunches.

He was holding a leash in his mouth.

Mad Dog

Here's a tip you can use if you are trying to make your way through a crowd of terrified people. Have a dog on a leash. Let the dog pretend to be a raging, maniacal, snapping, growling, snarling, potentially rabid killing machine. And suddenly the people become more terrified of the insane dog than they do of whatever emergency they are facing.

When Croc reappeared, at first we didn't know what to do with the leash hanging from his mouth. He dropped it on the floor at our feet and made a whimpering noise. We were confused.

"Hey, Croc, buddy," I said, "nice leash."

He scratched at the leash with his paws and whined again. Then he rolled over on it, rising to his feet, digging at it again with his forepaws.

Of course Angela figured it out. "I think he wants us to put it on him."

The lobby was still jam-packed with people and it didn't look like we were going anywhere soon. I reached down and fastened the leash to his collar. He nearly tore my arm off as soon as it was attached. Croc charged into the crowd, dragging me behind him. Angela barely had time to snatch my belt or we might have been separated in the crush of humanity.

Croc reared up on his hind legs, barking and howling. People took notice, and somehow space developed in front of us. Croc leaped forward. Whenever the crowd started to close in, Croc snarled and bared his teeth and we were given a wider berth.

"Sorry!" I yelled as we lunged past people. "He's a service dog. He's trying to get me to safety."

It would have taken us a long time to cross the huge lobby, but with Croc's help we were through the door and out on the street in minutes. Croc was still pulling me along. Apparently he took Boone's admonition that we get back to the intellimobile as fast as possible quite seriously. Though it was still crowded on the sidewalks, we had a little more room to maneuver.

There is no way to prepare yourself for what you witness in a full-on panic. Especially in a major city. With communications cut off so abruptly, Chicagoans had no idea if they would be attacked next. At every skyscraper we passed, streams of people emptied out into a vast river of humanity.

The police, firefighters, and first responders were doing a fantastic job of funneling people toward the trains and buses that they hoped would carry them to shelter. We saw a lot of panicked, frightened people, shoving and pushing, frantic in their efforts to get to safety.

Our cell phones beeped. Every once in a while, if you're

listening to the radio, you hear them talk about the Emergency Alert System. Radio stations have to test it every so often and when they do, you hear a loud tone for sixty seconds. It appeared to be back online. Except the service was only one way. Text messages flooded in. They said the city was preparing for the possibility of a potential chemical attack. The downtown area was thought to be a target. Emergency evacuation points were being established. Traffic was being rerouted to get people out of the city. More information flowed in, but there was no way to get a message out. No matter how we tried. Links appeared showing maps of the city with rendezvous points for evacuation to safe zones.

"They must take control of the cell towers," Angela said.

"I wonder why Boone hasn't let J.R. know that everything is okay here," I said, as Croc still jerked me along, determined to reach the intellimobile.

"I don't know," she said. "But he must have a reason. Maybe they want the cell to think something went wrong, like with the car bombs at Kitty Hawk. So the cell still thinks there's a chemical weapon that could still go off or . . . I don't know. But they must have their reasons."

Two more blocks and we were at the intellimobile. We pounded on the rear door panels and a few seconds later X-Ray poked his head out.

"Oh, it's you guys," he said. "Get in."

The three of us scrambled inside. I noticed X-Ray was holding a very big, very scary-looking pistol in his left hand, which he holstered inside the windbreaker he was wearing. Croc trotted up to the shotgun seat, like he always did. But this time, instead of curling up and going to sleep, he sat up on his haunches, alert and staring out the windshield.

"What's the word?" Angela asked X-Ray.

"Both of your parents are safe. Marie and Art did what they were trained for and got Roger and Blaze out of there as soon as the news about Atlanta and L.A. hit the airwaves. They also did it without tipping their hands that they're working for Boone. Malak is safe with Ziv. Someone showed up and tried to keep her in the park. We think it was set up so that it would look like the Leopard had accidentally been caught in her own attack. She took him out and Callaghan and Uly got him out of there. Boone wants you to stay here until Felix and Uly can get to the hotel. Then Roger and Blaze probably won't want you out of their sight for a while. The rest of us will rendezvous and figure out our next plan."

"Where is Ziv taking my mom?" Angela asked.

"I don't know yet. He won't contact us until he's at a safe location. He's probably got a dozen places to take her. But if she's been made, he'll be cautious until he knows she's safe. We'll hear from him when he decides it's time."

Angela stared off into space with a blank look on her face. I knew she was worried about her mom but I couldn't think of anything to say that would make her feel better.

"We don't know anything for sure, Angela," X-Ray said. He didn't sound too convincing.

"X-Ray, what happened in Atlanta and L.A.?" Angela asked. I was too overwhelmed to ask questions. Now that I felt relatively secure, I was trying to take everything in and finding it difficult. For the time being Angela seemed to have forgotten all about my *poofing* on the roof. I sure hadn't, though. My stomach wouldn't let me forget either.

X-Ray sighed. A look of terrible sadness came over his face.

"It's bad. There were gas attacks in Atlanta and L.A. at 8:46 a.m. this morning. We're not sure what type or how toxic it is yet. But it was . . . horrible." X-Ray's voice trailed off.

"How many people . . . ?" Angela started to say, but stopped because she couldn't bring herself to ask the question. But X-Ray knew what she was asking.

"Thousands. Maybe tens of thousands by the time all is said and done," he said.

Angela slammed her right fist into her left palm. Her face flushed red and her eyes looked like they had little flecks of lightning in them.

"We have got to stop these guys," she declared.

X-Ray looked at us. His kind face was sad and tired, and like all of Boone's crew, I wondered when was the last time he'd had a good night's sleep. He glared back at us and through the fatigue and exhaustion I saw fierce determination.

"Roger that," he said.

Changes

"What are we going to do, Mom?" I asked.

We were back in the hotel. Roger and Mom sat on a couch in the sitting room. Angela sat across from them. I couldn't stop pacing. Once again a deck of cards had appeared in my hands. But even cutting and shuffling wasn't calming me down this time.

We had stayed in the intellimobile until Felix and Uly showed up and escorted us back to our rooms. I changed my clothes and got rid of the cargo shorts with the bullet hole in them. That would be hard to explain. Then we waited for our parents to arrive. Waiting has never been my favorite thing. It felt like a lifetime until Marie knocked on our door and had us come join Mom and Roger in their suite. Felix and Uly left to do SOS stuff. Marie never moved more than four feet from the door and Art kept checking the windows and cracking his knuckles. I thought about how, just a few days ago, I never would have noticed anything unusual about his behavior. Now I understood he was checking each window, probably looking for anything suspicious. But mostly he was likely just ticked off that he wasn't out there busting a terrorist's head open. I had the feeling Art liked to break things in his off hours.

"Roger and I have talked about it. All air traffic has been temporarily grounded, but as soon as we can make it to Sausalito the venue has said they'll hold the concert. We've decided to continue with the tour as soon as normal travel is restored," she said. Roger nodded his head in agreement.

"Are you sure that's wise, Dad? Being out in a crowded venue? Exposing yourself like that?" Angela asked. There had still been no word from Ziv or Malak, so Angela was quiet and . . . I'd say the word was angry. Not at her dad or me or anybody. Maybe just mad at the world. Right now all this stuff was happening and every time it seemed we might be close to ending it—and she could finally reunite with her mom— something else really bad happened and kept them apart.

Roger looked at my mom for a moment before he answered.

"I don't know, honey," he said. "The world is . . . it's just upside down right now. But Blaze and I talked about it. We're going to keep the tour going. We're going to keep raising money for the victims. We will not let a bunch of cowardly thugs dictate how we live our lives."

"What if no one comes to the concerts?" I asked. "Because they're too afraid."

"Then they don't come," Mom replied. "We can't control what other people do. But we can control how we react to it. If people don't show up, they don't show up. We're still playing."

I knew better than to argue with her. Once Mom had made up her mind, no one was going to convince her otherwise. Except for the nagging issue that the ghost cell seemed to keep following us around. But maybe now that Buddy T. was gone, they wouldn't have any insider information to use against us.

"Mom, Roger," I said. "If it matters at all, I think you're doing the right thing."

"Me, too," Angela said. I knew she was still worried and scared for Malak. But even scared, worried Angela knew they were right.

"It matters," my mom said. I even think she got a little teary-eyed. "It matters a lot."

My cell phone chirped.

"It's Boone," I said. "Hello?"

"Hey, Q, are you with your folks?"

"Yes."

"Do me a favor and put me on speaker," he said.

I did as he asked and set the phone on the table in front of the couch.

"Boone?" Mom asked. "Is everything all right?"

"Purty near," he said, with the familiar country-boy drawl he used when he was in roadie mode. "You probably heard all the flights have been canceled for now. We managed to get all the equipment loaded on the truck. Anyhow, I just heard from Heather. She's gonna have her plane fueled up and ready to go as soon as it's okay to fly. Luckily we had the second truck already on the road. You still plannin' to play?"

"Boone, if we can get there, we're playing," Mom answered.

"That's what I figured. Well, the other truck has already arrived, so you got equipment and everything you need. I guess we just gotta get you and the rest of the crew there, is all."

"We'll get there somehow," Mom said. "I have a feeling."

"Me, too," Boone said. "Hey, Q and Angela?"

"Yeah?" we asked.

"Since y'all are with your mom and dad, I'll catch up with you once we're in California. If I can get a flight, that is. I gotta stay behind and figure out how to get all the gear to the next stop. It's kind of chaos right now. But Pat Callaghan's gonna go with you once the flight restrictions get lifted. That work for you and Roger and Blaze?"

"Sure," Mom said.

"All right," Boone said. "I guess I'll see y'all in California."

I knew we would.

I also knew he wouldn't be flying there.

Boone ended the call and Angela and I went back to our rooms. We would have to wait around until we found out when the flight grounding would be lifted.

"Q, I've got about a million questions," she said. "But the most important one is, are you all right?"

"I think so. I mean I don't feel sick or anything anymore."

"Q, how . . . what . . . did you really do what Boone does? Did I really see what I thought I saw?"

"Angela, I wish I knew how to answer that. I looked up and saw a laser dot on your forehead. You were milliseconds from getting shot. And the next thing I knew, I'd pushed you out of the way. Then Croc threw the guy off the roof. After that, I barfed."

"Did you feel anything?"

"Not until afterward. I had a headache and got sick to my stomach. Like I'd ridden Space Mountain at Disneyland twenty times after eating a double order of chili cheese fries. Which reminds me. Are you hungry?"

I wasn't changing the subject. I *was* hungry.

"Don't change the subject. Do you think Boone had anything to do with it?"

"Well, obviously he did because I think I did the exact thing he and Croc do."

"I mean, do you think he gives off a field of energy or something? And you figured out how to tap into it?"

"I don't know."

"Can you do it again?"

"No way! Okay, at first, I thought—cool illusion or trick or whatever. But then it happened. And it wasn't fun. It was kind of scary, actually. And I've been thinking about it. Suppose it's like running really fast somewhere. What if I hadn't stopped and pushed you out of the way? What if I'd run right off the roof?"

"But you didn't. So you must have some control over it."

"I'm not taking any chances. Not unless I'm someplace on the ground, with wide-open spaces where I won't run into a tree or something."

"But what happens if you don't have control over it? And like you say, something dangerous happens? Don't you think we should talk to Boone?"

"Yes. Probably. But there's a big giant emergency going on

and he's kind of busy. So I'm just going to stay calm and try to avoid blinking my eyes and ending up in front of a train or something. Then I'll talk to Boone when we get to California."

Angela didn't know what to say; she did her chewing on her lip thing, which meant she probably had a lot to say, but wasn't going to say it. I just let it pass. I was still confused and a little afraid.

I lay down on the bed and shuffled and cut my deck of cards. Just to be sure, I blinked my eyes. Several times.

But I stayed there on the bed. Not moving. And I was glad.

Resolve

There was one number Boone didn't store in his phone. He
had it memorized. Someone who had been around as long as
Boone had, who'd done the things he did, had enemies. If he
ever lost his phone, he didn't need someone calling up J.R. on
a number only a handful of people in the world had access to.
Boone knew J.R. would be up to his ears in this crisis so he'd
waited as long as he could before he called.

When he dialed, J. R. Culpepper answered on the first
ring. Almost like he was waiting for Boone's call. And he
didn't sound happy.

"I'm a little busy, Boone."

"I know. I just need a couple things."

"You can't have a satellite. They're all tasked right now."

"I know. Do you have everyone looking for Buddy T.?"

"Everyone I can spare. There's a lot going on, in case you
haven't heard. I've looked through the file. We didn't find
anything more than your guy did. Buddy T. is a ghost. I'll find
a way to get your team to California as fast as possible and you

find this guy. But it's going to be a couple of days. Only fighter jets are going up right now."

"We'll find him. Buddy can run all he wants. He's never had to worry about being hunted before. He's smart. But he's gone soft. He can't fly either. If I had to guess, I'd bet he took a train. Lot less scrutiny on a train. If you can, you might have people check the westbound passenger trains. Slow 'em up a little. Trains are delayed all the time anyway."

"I can do that. But apparently he hasn't gone soft enough. If it hadn't been for you he would have killed a lot more people."

"Did they ever find out what the chemical was?" Boone asked.

"Not yet. Something the squints at Quantico and Langley haven't seen before. But it's bad . . . Boone. What you did in Chicago? With the wind there? Who knows how many you saved?"

"I had help."

"Well, they're going to get a medal when this is over."

"No. No, they're not. They're going to school."

"Are you kidding me? Angela and Q were there on this?"

"Yep. Q figured it out. They're smart kids. But once this is over, I want them to go back to normal. Although you might want to consider Angela for director of the Secret Service before your term is up. She's going to be heard from someday. And Q, too. That kid is way smart. He just doesn't want anyone to know it."

"Wow. If Malak knew she'd be incredibly proud. Then she'd shoot you in the knee for putting Angela in danger."

"Don't I know it."

"Look, Boone, national emergency here. I've got to address the nation in thirty minutes. What do you need?"

"I'll need a C-5 Galaxy cargo plane at Great Lakes Naval Station to haul the coach and our other vehicles to San Francisco. And when you cancel the no-fly order, Heather Hughes has a corporate jet here in Chicago, at Midway airport. Let them be one of the first ones out of here."

"Roger on the C-5. But what's the deal on the corporate jet?"

"I just need to get Q and Angela to California. We're close, J.R. I always thought Angela was the key to this. That she unknowingly had something, some memento with a secret code or something from Malak when she was 'dead,' that the cell wanted. But now I'm not so sure that's the case anymore."

"Why?"

"Because of Q. Something isn't adding up. Not since the cell took him prisoner in San Antonio. And I don't want either of them out of my sight, if I can help it. And he did something today that I've only seen one other person do."

"What was it?"

"Not ready to talk about that yet."

"I could order you to tell me."

"You could. But I don't work for you. NOC. No Official Cover. Remember?"

"All right, Boone. You play it your way. But try not to get a couple of celebrities' kids killed in the middle of this. After all the truly horrible things that have happened today . . . I don't want this to sound selfish. But I've got enough explaining to

do. *Please* tell me you're going to bring these guys down.
This . . ."

J. R. Culpepper stopped speaking, but Boone could hear
the quivering emotion in his voice. Shortly he would go on
camera. He would reassure the American people. He would
be strong and resolute. But the enormity of the tragedy was
tearing at his heart. J.R. was one of the few politicians Boone
knew who always thought of people first and politics second.

"Copy that. Goodbye, J.R."

But President J. R. Culpepper had already hung up.

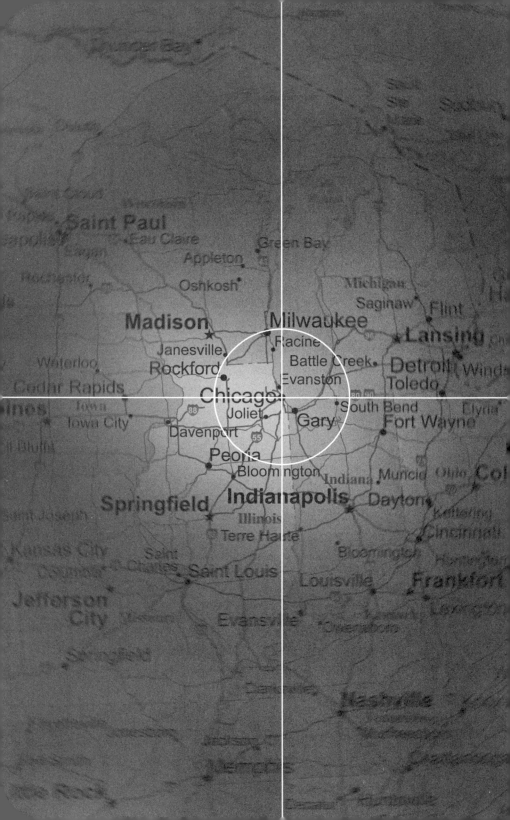

MONDAY, SEPTEMBER 15 ⟩

7:00 a.m. to 9:00 a.m. CST

Out of Options

We couldn't get a flight out for four days. Everything stayed grounded. We spent our time in the hotel, mostly with Mom and Roger. We played board games, Roger played his guitar a lot, and they both sang. Art kept pacing back and forth in front of the windows, cracking his knuckles.

Angela and I had our stuff packed so we could be ready to go at a moment's notice. It wasn't all that hard since we didn't carry much with us. Most of our clothes and other gear stayed on the coach. But we each had a suitcase and our backpacks ready.

It's funny what you think of in the middle of a crisis. I remembered running away from all of the terrified hordes of people in the Hancock building. But I also remembered something else you frequently see in an emergency. It's people behaving at their best. We'd seen taxi drivers hollering at running people to get in and be taken to the evacuation points for no charge. Drivers in all types of vehicles stopped to beckon those on foot to hitch rides. I remembered a guy driving an empty panel truck pulled over and jumped out of the cab. He lifted the back door and encouraged people to hop aboard until he had as many passengers as he could safely carry. Then he drove off.

We passed small stores where the employees handed out bottles of water and energy drinks to those rushing by—and collecting no payment while they did it. People who had fallen, tripped, or were injured in the rush were helped to their feet or given first aid by total strangers.

As we ran that day, as scared as I was, it made me think. What we saw showed why the cell was never going to win. Despite their fanaticism, terrorists always fail. No matter how hard you try to knock us down, we keep getting up. We might be scared or frightened temporarily. But ultimately we keep coming back. We will not stop.

And that day had been one I'd soon like to forget. But as I've learned, in the spy game, a lot of your time is spent waiting. Waiting is bad for me. It gives me time to think. Like about what happened to me on the roof. The fact that all those people died. How it could have been worse if we hadn't been there. So my mind races, which leads to the fidgeting.

I knew I was making Angela antsy and was about to apologize for driving her nuts when her cell phone chirped.

The change in her face as she read the text was remarkable. She smiled and visibly relaxed. She was sitting on the couch and she put her elbows on her knees. It was almost refreshing. Angela had been so wound up since Kitty Hawk I was actually worried about her health. And also, that she might get horked off and kick me in the face if I made a dumb joke or practiced with my cards too much.

"What is it?" I said.

"It's from Ziv."

I waited for her to tell me what the text said. And waited. And waited some more.

"Uh. Angela?"

Still nothing.

"Angela?"

"Oh. What?"

"You got a text?"

"Yes! I did!"

"You sound excited. Want to tell me who it was from?"

"What? Oh, it's from Ziv."

"Yes. So you said."

"My mom. She's okay. She's with him. At least I think so. Ziv's texts are very . . . cryptic."

"What does it say?"

" 'The Leopard sleeps.' "

"That's it?"

"Yeah. But that's good, right?"

"I think so."

Truth was, I didn't know. Boone said Ziv took Malak from the park. But it's possible they could have run into trouble during their escape. Maybe the cell had other operatives watching and they attacked them as they were leaving. Maybe Agent Callaghan and the others didn't know about it. She could be wounded. Having met Ziv, though, I thought he could handle any kind of trouble that came along. So they could also be somewhere eating chili cheese fries. Angela was right. Ziv was cryptic. I think he did it on purpose. Also, thinking about chili cheese fries reminded me again that I was still hungry. Nerves and national emergencies make me hungry. I can't help it.

"I think it means she's okay. Boone would have told us otherwise. I'm guessing your mom made Ziv text to reassure you. Knowing your mom, she probably made him do it at gunpoint."

Angela chuckled at that. It was good to hear her laughing again.

"Are you hungry?" I asked.

"As a matter of fact, I am."

We went to the suite. Mom cupped my face with her hands when we walked in. She'd been doing it a lot ever since what happened four days ago.

"Are you two okay?" she asked.

"We're fine, Mom. It'll be okay."

"Art just went down to the restaurant to see if he could scrounge up some food. The hotel is obviously running on a skeleton staff. You guys must be starved."

"It's okay," I said. And it really was. I felt a little ashamed. Thousands of my fellow citizens were killed or injured and I was worrying about getting something to eat.

"Also there's news. We just got word. Flights in cities except New York and L.A. are allowed to take off. The jet will be fueled up and ready to go in a couple hours." Roger stood behind Mom, looking at the floor, the ceiling, everywhere but at me and Angela.

I was getting itchy.

"Mom, what's wrong? You haven't decided to cancel the tour or something, have you?" I asked.

"No, it's not that. . . ." Mom was usually pretty straightforward.

"Angela, Q," Roger said. "Blaze and I have been talking about it. Like we said, we're going to go on with the tour, terrorists or no terrorists. But we're not going to take unnecessary risks. So we've decided that when we get back to California, we're enrolling you in boarding school. You'll be safe."

"What?" Angela said. "Why? You can't do this!"

"It's already done, sweetie," my mom said. "There are just some things we're not willing to leave to chance. We have an obligation to finish our tour and do our jobs. But that doesn't mean we have to expose you to danger."

"Mom!" I said. "I don't want to go to boarding school! We've done our homework, we've kept our bargain! This isn't fair!"

"Q, I know you're upset, but this attack changes—"

"Yeah. I'm upset. We did everything you asked. And now you're just going to change the rules?"

"Q, that's not fair," Roger said. "Your mother has—"

"Don't tell me what my mother has done!" I yelled at Roger. "You're not my dad. Stop trying to pretend like you are!" I turned around and stalked out of the suite and went back to my room.

My mom hollered after me, "Q! Come back here! And don't you speak to Roger like that—"

But her words were cut off by the sound of the slamming

door. I actually felt like I would *poof* away if could. I closed my
eyes and concentrated. When I opened them I was still alone
in my room.

Nothing.

MONDAY, SEPTEMBER 15   >

12 noon to 5:30 p.m. PST

The Show Must Go On

We took off from Midway airport and circled out over Lake Michigan. If you've ever seen it up close, it looks like an ocean, not a lake. Our flight plan took us north and the city skyline was on the left side of the aircraft.

I was sitting in the very back seat on the left. Before we boarded, Mom caught up with me and chewed me out pretty good for smarting off to Roger. She made me apologize. Which I did. But I still wasn't happy about the whole boarding-school thing. I know there were bigger issues at stake. I know they were doing what they thought was best. But I felt that leaving the tour would take us away from helping Boone take down the cell. And the thought of being so close and not able to finish it just pushed me over the edge.

Angela left me alone at first, but eventually she came and sat down across from me. She was chewing on her lip. Might as well get it over with.

"Say it," I said.

"What?"

I sighed.

"We've been over this. You're doing the lip thing again."

"I just want to know if you're okay. You've been . . . I know you've been worried about me. Because I've been so freaked about finding out about my mom being alive and her being in danger and stuff. You're a good guy, Q. But you've got your own issues going on. If you want to talk about what happened . . ."

"I don't."

"Why?"

"Because I don't. I haven't—what's the word? Processed it yet. But there is one thing that is bothering me. Why didn't Boone take the guy out?"

"What do mean? Maybe he didn't see what was happening."

"Come on, Angela. The guy is like some kind of freaky ninja. On the island at Kitty Hawk he was all over the place. Do you really think he couldn't have taken down a single shooter? Right before we got on the elevator, I asked him if he couldn't just *poof* up to the roof. He said 'not yet' or 'not right now' or something. And he was all sweaty and icky-looking."

"Maybe he found the weapon and was trying to disarm it first."

Leave it to Angela to bring up a point I hadn't considered. I suppose he could have been busy with the chemical device. But still . . .

"Q, look, I know you've got to be weirded out by this. And it would help to be able to talk with Boone about it. And as many questions as I have for him, I would imagine you have even more. Have you considered that maybe you just got to me first? Maybe Boone was just getting ready to *poof* and save me or toss the gunman off the roof and he saw you do it first? And now he's just as confused as you are. Or, if he was sweaty and icky, like you said, maybe his ability has some kind of limit."

I didn't say anything. I hadn't thought of that either. For whatever reason, having experienced Boone's little magic trick for myself was freaking me out. And after I *poofed*, I got sick. Maybe it takes something out of you when you do it and Boone has just learned to control it somehow. So many questions.

I just stared out the window. We were gaining altitude but down below us I could see a big cargo plane taking off from an airstrip. It was huge. Big enough to carry a bus. Or two. It looked like a military aircraft. I guess air traffic was getting back to normal after the attack.

Angela knew when I didn't want to talk anymore. So she remained quiet and opened her laptop and left me alone to think.

And that's what I did. All the way to California. Even when we had to stop and refuel in Montana, I didn't get off the plane. I thought about everything. From the time I literally stumbled over Boone in the desert to *poofing* on top of a Chicago skyscraper. I thought about the bombing in Washington, D.C. Then I remembered how we stopped the ghost cell in San Antonio and Chicago. But no matter what we did, they still managed to hurt people in Atlanta, Paris, and L.A.

And for some reason, that made me think of Speed. My real dad. He lived in L.A. I wondered if he was okay.

"Hey, Angela," I said. She looked up at me from her computer screen. No doubt she was using whatever down time we might have to study something.

"Yeah?"

"You know that tracker thing Boone put in my dad's boot?"

"Yeah."

"Can you pull up that program on your laptop? See where he is?"

Angela looked at me for a few brief seconds. Her hands worked the keyboard.

"The signal shows it's coming from Key West, in the Florida Keys," she said.

She turned the screen around so I could see it. It showed a map of southern Florida. Way out in the Keys a red dot blinked.

"Thanks," I said, "I appreciate it."

Speed had really gone to the Keys. Just like he said he would. It was probably the first true thing he'd ever told me in my life. Of course he waited until he and my mom were divorced to say it. But at least he was okay.

Angela was quiet all the way until we landed at the San Francisco airport. Mom and Roger had sat in the front of the plane with Heather the entire time. I knew Mom was just giving me space. I also knew the three of them were talking about nothing else but the attacks and what had happened with Buddy T. Why hadn't he come back? If only they knew what we knew.

Marie and Art sat in the middle. Marie had her ever-present look of serenity on her face. I knew she could probably kill someone seven different ways with just her thumb. But no one would ever see it coming. Art was a little more intense. Unlike Marie, Art's face was not serene. His jaw was clenched and his eyes were clear and bright. I was pretty sure he wanted to get in on the action. Find a terrorist he could punch in the head several times. But Boone picked and trained his people very well. I knew Mom and Roger were safe with Marie and Art watching them.

We landed in a part of the airport reserved for private craft. The inside of the terminal looked a lot like a regular terminal, only not as big. It had less security, and big glass windows you could look out of. Lots of other planes were landing and taxiing around. Then I saw it. About three hundred yards away was a hangar area for military aircraft. A giant cargo plane was parked on the tarmac. The back end of it was opened up and a huge ramp descended from the inside. A Marathon coach rolled down the ramp. It looked a lot like ours. Probably because it had a big "Match" logo on the side. Then a Range Rover rolled down the ramp. Followed by the intellimobile. It was ours! Uh-oh. And Mom and Roger were standing right there. Their backs were to the window but they could turn around at any second. If they spotted the coach and recognized it, we were in for a lot of questions. Starting with why their coach was being unloaded from a military aircraft.

I caught Art's attention and nodded out the window. He followed my gaze and his eyes went wide. We had to get

Mom and Roger and Heather out of there. And fast. But how?
I saw a little kiosk across the terminal that sold magazines,
sodas, and candy bars. Quickly, I sped over and rummaged
through my cargo pants until I found enough change to buy a
Kit Kat bar. I hustled back to a spot twenty feet from the group
and stood so that I was facing the window. Then I made a big
loud show of ripping open the wrapping and snapping off a
piece of chocolate. I took a big bite. It was like heaven on my
tongue.

Angela noticed me first and her mouth made an O shape.
"Q?" she said. "What–?"

I shushed her.

The commotion attracted Mom's and Roger's attention.
Roger looked at the candy bar, then at me. His expression
was not pleasant.

"Q!" My mom said. She stomped over to me. "What are
you doing?"

"Eating a candy bar," I said. "It was a long flight."

"You know we don't eat like that anymore. That's very
disrespectful to Roger. What has gotten into you?" she asked.

"Right now, chocolate. And since I've got to go to *boarding
school*, I feel like I should at least get to eat what I want," I said.

"Q! I know you're not happy about this decision. But it's
been made. So you'll just have to accept it. This isn't like you.
And no matter how mad you are, you don't get to be rude to
Roger. He's done nothing to deserve it. Now you throw that
out right now!" she said.

"All right, fine," I said.

I stalked off toward a trash can that was about fifty feet

away. As I did, I glanced out the window. The three vehicles were pulling away. I kept moving toward the trash can and all eyes in the group were on me. Mom followed along in lockstep.

When I reached the trash can she put her hand on my arm. She had placed herself between me and Roger.

"Q, before you throw that away give me a piece, will you? This diet we're on? I'm starving."

Chinese Food

Union Square in San Francisco was its usual buzz of activity. Commuters on their way to work rushed by with briefcases and cups of coffee in hand. Street performers and homeless people competed for spare change. No one noticed an older, gray-haired bearded man and his aging dog materialize on a previously empty bench.

Boone leaned forward and put his arms on his knees. His entire body ached and he felt weak and dizzy. His breathing was labored and it took him several minutes to catch his breath. No one stopped to ask him if he was okay. People passed by without noticing him at all. In a city like San Francisco an old man like Boone was invisible.

Croc was lying at his feet and finally rose slowly, pawing at Boone's leg as he did.

"I know, boy," Boone said. As he reached down to stroke the dog's head the muscles in his arm cramped and he groaned with the effort. "It's getting harder for me every time, isn't it?"

Croc lay back down on the ground, resting his head on

Boone's foot.

"I think that's the last one for a while. Going to take some time to build up the energy again, don't you think?"

Croc raised his head to look at Boone and the old man could swear the dog nodded in agreement.

"What would I do without you?" he said with a sigh. "We've got to get moving, pal. There's a lot to do. People are depending on us."

The morning fog had burned off and the sun was bright in the sky. Boone leaned back on the bench. He let the sun warm his face. It was a glorious day. The kind of day he would enjoy if he didn't feel so weak.

Croc whined.

"I know. You're hungry. Just a few more minutes, buddy."

Finally Boone felt like he had the strength to stand and walk.

Croc barked and huffed at his feet, standing now, his tail wagging.

"Seriously? Chinese food? This early? You know what Chinese does to your--"

Croc barked, louder this time. Interrupting him.

"All right, all right . . . you win. Chinese it is. But absolutely no kung pao chicken."

Croc whined.

"No. Way."

Boone stood and stretched. With Croc at his side, he headed for Chinatown.

Disappearing into the crowd.

Roland Smith

Roland Smith is a *New York Times* best-selling author of eighteen novels for young readers and more than a dozen nonfiction titles and picture books. Raised in the music business, Smith has incorporated his experience into the *I,Q* series. When he's not at home writing, Smith spends a good part of the year speaking with students at schools around the country. Learn more about the *I,Q* books at www.iqtheseries.com. Learn more about Roland Smith at www.rolandsmith.com.

Michael P. Spradlin

New York Times best-selling author Michael P. Spradlin has
written more than twenty books for children and adults. He
is the author of the *Killer Species* series and the international
best-selling *The Youngest Templar* trilogy. He lives in Michigan
and can be visited on the Web at michaelspradlin.com.

www.IQtheSeries.com